A Talent For Rescue

Three Stories in the Salvage Title Universe

Robert E. Hampson

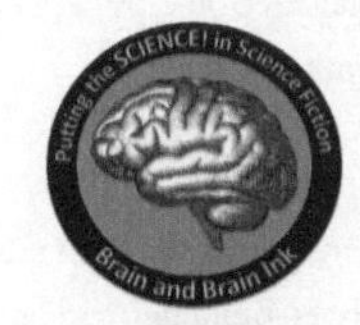

Brain and Brain Ink

Contents

For Ruann, the love of my life; for Mom, my first fan; and for Dad, my hero and role model.

Additional Copyright Information

This book is a work of fiction, and any resemblance to persons, living or dead, or places, events, or locales is purely coincidental. The characters are productions of the author's imagination and used fictitiously.

These stories take place in Kevin Steverson's *Salvage Title* Universe. All rights to that universe and setting are retained by Kevin Steverson and Chris Kennedy Publishing.

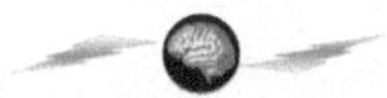

"The Suit" by Robert E. Hampson, copyright 2019 by Robert E. Hampson. First appeared in *Salvage Conquest: Tales from the Salvage Title Universe*, edited by Chris Kennedy & Kevin Steverson, published by Theogony Books, Chris Kennedy Publishing.

"Cheating the Odds" by Robert E. Hampson, copyright 2020 by Robert E. Hampson. First appeared in *Through the Gate: More Tales from the Salvage Title Universe (The Coalition Book 3)*, edited by Chris Kennedy & Kevin Steverson, published by Theogony Books, Chris Kennedy Publishing.

"Rescue Ops" by Robert E. Hampson, copyright 2021 by Robert E. Hampson. First appeared in *It Takes All Kinds (The Coalition Book 9)* edited by Kevin Steverson and Chris Kennedy, published by Theogony Books, Chris Kennedy Publishing.

Cover art by Robert E. Hampson. A portion of the artwork was derived from Midjourney.AI (paid user).

THE SUIT

Authors note: This is my first story written in the Salvage Title Universe. When I first read Kevin Steverson's book <u>Salvage Title</u>, I was struck by how the characters reminded me of the old Boy's Life tales from my youth. The stories emphasized curiosity, ingenuity, self-sufficiency, and an overall positive view of the world. Thus, Pete, Orlin, Jerry, and Jinx are based on the ideal of Scouting when I was growing up. Here then, is the first tale of Pete Ekil, a young man with a talent...for rescue.

"So, what are you going to do for your Maker Merit Badge?" Orlin was digging through the pile of discarded mech components. He'd told his companions all about his plans to build his own mech, 'just like Harmon Tomeral' and was now trying to figure out how much competition he was going to have from the other members of his patrol. Even though Tomeral had long left the Tretra system, he was still a hero, particularly on Joth, where he'd grown up under circumstances much like Orlin and his friends.

"I don't know," replied Pettekil—Pete to his friends—flipping his tail back and forth with nervous energy. "I think everyone wants to copy him and build mechs. I want to do something different." He turned back to his desultory sorting through burnt motivators, exhausted power cells and damaged sensors. "There's nothing of interest in this junk pile."

"We want to build..." started Jerry.

"... a fighter!" finished Jinx. The twins usually finished each other's sentences. They often talked about becoming fighter pilots because they assumed that their ability to coordinate their actions would provide an advantage in combat.

"Of course you do," said Orlin with a sigh of resignation. "It's all you two ever talk about."

"Hey J—" called Jerry.

"Yeah, J—" replied Jinx.

"There's a thruster..."

"...over here.."

"Wow, two..."

"...at a time? How lucky—"

"—is that?" completed Jinx

"Can you two please stop that?" asked Pete. "Do you know how annoying that is? Especially when the rest of us haven't found jack... uh... diddly."

"Just because—"

"—you can't look with four eyes—"

"—doesn't mean we can't!"

The irony was that 'Pete' was a Caldivar, an anteater-like creature with three eyes. He had an advantage over the human twins, and even Orlin, who was a lizard-like Prithmar. Joth was home to many races, and it was not uncommon for them to mix in both social and occupational settings. The four boys were all in the same Troop, and even the same Patrol—the Crockables, named for a leathery-winged scavenger bird common to the vast deserts of Joth.

"You have one more eye than I have, so I wouldn't call that much of an advantage..." he started, but was interrupted by Orlin.

"A-HA! Got another knee joint, here. Now I just need a couple of hip joints and the lower limbs are set."

"You guys have all the luck," Pete grumped.

"Alright guys. The troop as a whole is going to be working on the Maker Merit Badge this month. Since you're all on school break for the next three weeks, you should be able to spend all the time you need during that time period. Remember, merit badge rules say that you can work individually, or in teams up to the size of a patrol, however, to earn the badge, your team-mates must agree that you contributed significantly to the overall project. I've arranged for you to have access to the Farnog Corp printers, and the Rinto Scrap Yard will let you pick through the unsorted salvage. The rest of it is up to you. Build it, program it, salvage it... Just make sure that it is a functioning device of value to Joth society, because we'll be entering them in the Joth Maker Faire next month."

Troopmaster Zentto was Prithmar, like about one-third of the kids in the troop. Another third were human, and the remainder was a mix of Caldivar, Yalteen, Pikith and even a couple of Leethog. Xenophobia was rare on Joth given the number of different races present on the desert-like world. The variety also made the Crockables' troop quite successful in the various planet wide youth competitions like the Maker Faire. Residents of Joth were always inventive and self-reliant, but the popularity of build-it-yourself projects and competitions had really taken off after Joth's favorite son, Harmon Tomeral, had won the Top Fleet Marine competition. The fact that Tomeral ended up saving the entire system from the Squilla hadn't hurt either. Inventive, unorthodox, self-reliant, heroic—Tomeral was an example to all. Thanks to his example, every young resident of Joth wanted to be the next to make their mark on the universe.

The only problem was that Pete still didn't know what he was making for the competition. Orlin had most of an exoskeleton together and was starting to fashion armor plates. Even if it wasn't a full mecha, he'd already proven its worth by using the augmented strength to improve the searches in the salvage yard. Jerry and Jinx had affixed their thrusters and motors to a hover frame that the quartet used to transport their finds back to the workspace that the troop had arranged for their members to finish projects. The other three were well on their way to completing the merit badge and even had a chance of scoring well at the Maker Faire. Pete was the only one without a project of his own.

Of course, he could always work with his patrol-mates on their projects. He was helping them with programming anyway, so there was no question but that he was contributing significantly. It's just that he wanted something of his own.

"Hey, what's this—" started Jerry

"—it looks like armor—"

"—but soft—"

"—and no joints," ended Jinx.

The device in question did look vaguely like something a bipedal could wear. There were four tubes roughly the size and shape of humanoid arms and legs. There was also a much larger, clamshell that looked like it would fit the torso of Yalteen. It was much too large for a human, let alone a Caldivar or Human. There didn't seem to be anything joining the separate pieces into a suit or armor, although there were some damaged tubes that <u>might</u> have connected the various pieces at one time. There was also no evidence of a helmet or joint protection.

"If it's a Mecha, it's missing anything practical," observed Orlin. "I suppose it might be some sort of an add-on, like ablative armor."

"Not armor—"

"—too soft." Jinx held up one of the tubes. It might have been a sleeve, with a semi-flexible elbow joint, but Pete agreed, it was much too soft. The material was almost a fabric, it seemed as if the only reason it even held its shape was more tubing inside.

"Could it be some sort of reactive material that can be programmed to be rigid in one state and flexible in another?" Orlin had picked up another of the sleeves. This one bore a similarity to a leg, with a large diameter opening at one end, a narrow opening at the other, and once again, a slight flex where a knee joint might be located.

"If that's the case—"

"—where are the shoulders—"

"—and hips?"

"You would think—"

"—that it would be important—"

"—to protect them, too!"

"If it's programmable, there should be a controller. Look around for anything that looks like a processor that has those tubes coming out of it. We'll take it back with us and I'll hook it up and see what it does. If we can figure it out, maybe Orlin can add it to his exoskeleton." Pete might not have a project of his own, but if he could figure out programmable armor for Orlin's mecha, that would be a worthwhile contribution. "Jinx, Jer, help me put this on the H-frame."

"Here is a box—"

"—the same shape—"

"—as the discoloration—"

"—on the 'chest.'"

Sure enough, the object appeared to be some sort of computer processor, and was exactly the same size and shape as a corresponding discolored place on the front of the clamshell. It even had indications of wiring connectors in locations that lined up between the two pieces. It didn't make sense to put a controller right on the front of armor where it would be the first thing hit. Maybe there was more to this "armor" than met the eye. Was there a reason why the builders weren't worried about the exposed control panel? Was it some form of energy shield?

Pete's imagination began to race. Maybe he wouldn't have to treat this as simply a part of Orlin's mecha. Maybe he could make this on his own.

The main workshop was noisy. Orlin alternated between heating metal plates in an electroforge and hammering them on an archaic iron anvil to make hardened plates that would cover key components of his mecha. He'd decided to proceed with hip, shoulder and neck armor while Pete tried to figure out the mysterious components they'd pulled out of the salvage yard. Jerry and Jinx were arguing in their strange style while the remounted the hover thrusters with vectored nozzles to transition from vertical lift to forward thrust.

Meanwhile, Pete worked in the quieter clean-room to one side of the work-shop, cleaning and rebuilding the wiring connections between the controller, torso and limbs of the strange armor. The most unusual feature of the device was that the tubing appeared to be able to fill with some form of fluid to form a rigid frame. Unfortunately, he hadn't figured out if there was a way to make the fabric itself become less flexible.

Perhaps it had something to do with what fluid was pumped into the tubes? Maybe this wasn't armor. Was it a cooling system? If so, why did it even need the fabric covering?

So far, he'd only worked with one of the suit limbs, experimenting with providing electrical current, then air pressure to the tubing, then fluid pressure in the form of water, hydraulic oil and liquid refrigerant. None of them seemed to make a difference, but he hadn't tried hooking up the complete system yet.

Still, before doing that, he needed to figure out what fluid the suit used. There was one long piece of tubing that had been attached to the clamshell at shoulder height, if there was still some trace in there, perhaps he could have someone analyze it.

"This is unusual; you don't see these molecules very often. Lots of fluorine and carbon, usually called a 'perfluorocarbon.'" Pete's cousin Bereketil showed him the diagram on the slate of a number of carbon molecules bonded to fluoride molecules. "Breck" was a graduate student in Materials Engineering at the new branch of the Tretrayon Academy that had opened on Joth in the last few years. It didn't completely eliminate the history of inferior treatment of Joth and its citizens by the system capital, but it was a start.

"Wasn't that used in refrigeration units? So this _is_ some kind of cooling suit." Pete picked up the tubing he'd asked his older cousin to analyze for him.

"Not really. Refrigerants usually contained chlorine as well. Chlorofluoro-carbons were banned millennia again, and frankly, there's better ways to cool than letting a liquid evaporate, absorbing heat, then compressing it back to a liquid and venting the heat somewhere else. No, there were several other uses as well, such as fire suppressants and electrical insulation. If it was pumped through your suit, perhaps it was worn by shipboard damage control. It would probably be fire-proof and shock-proof." Breck tapped on his slate some more. "Oh, this is interesting." He showed Pete a diagram of a molecule that looked like two six-sided rings that shared a side. "Perfluorodecalin. Ten carbons, eighteen fluorines. There were some attempts on Earth at using for a blood substitute."

"For humans, then. That won't help me much."

"Actually, it helps carry oxygen, so most races with closed circulatory systems can use it." Breck handed the slate over to Pete. "Show me those pictures you took again."

Pete placed his own slate on top of his cousin's and initiated the transfer, then pocketed his own and handed Breck's slate back to him. "That's what we're calling the torso unit. It looks like it would fit down over a neck and then close at the sides."

"Big, isn't it? Not human sized. Not Caldivar and certainly not Prithmar. Yalteen?"

"Tall enough, but much bigger in the chest. More like the Withaloo who settled in Salvage." Pete tapped the slate again. "These are the sleeves. Near as I can tell there are two fluid tubes and a wiring harness supposed to connect each one to the torso unit. There's also four wiring connectors—one at each corner—connecting the control unit to the torso. Those were intact, and I have just about gotten them clean enough to re-attach."

"Wait, how much of this have you done on your own? You're still in Upper School, right?"

"Actually, Jerry and Jinx's father helped a bit with the electrical. You know we do this for fun in the Troop, right?"

"I remember you took apart my watch when you were just a pup. I never did get it to synch back up with my slate after that."

"Um. I've <u>built</u> watches, since then, Breck. From a kit, true, but they work."

"Huh. Think you can do something with this one, then?" Breck extended a claw and popped the catch on a black band he wore around one leathery wrist. "It hasn't worked right since I started working in this lab."

Pete took the watch and held it up to look closely with his lower, left eye, the one he usually used for fine detail. "You know this has been etched, right? Looks like acid of some sort."

"Oh, damn. That's what it was. I'm still catching grief from the professor about that spill. Okay, never mind." He held out a paw to take the watch back but Pete kept it just out of reach.

"Actually, it's fixable. I can open it up, clean the moly's, lay down new traces and print a new case for it. I owe for doing this, at least." He nodded toward the bench-top analyzer Breck had used to analyze the residual fluid in the tubing.

"Hey, thanks, cuz. This? This was no trouble, and I appreciate the watch. Good luck figuring out what your suit does."

"Pete—"

"—did you notice—"

"—these ports—"

"—on the back?"

Jerry and Jinx had the torso of Pete's "firefighter suit" in a cabinet where it could be sprayed with a fine abrasive to remove contaminants and polish metallic surfaces. Each of the twins pointed to a line of small fittings along each side of the back plate. They had previously been covered in a hard crust of some sort of resinous material. The boys had offered to let him use the cleaning chamber once they finished cleaning their thruster nozzles. They must have finished early, because the suit fittings positively shone with a blue-green glimmer in the artificial lighting of the shop.

"You guys are done with the nozzles?"

"Well actually—"

"—one of them was so worn—"

"—the abrasive cut a hole—"

"—right through the chamber wall—"

"—we need to go—"

"—back and find a new one—"

"—so we decided to—"

"—help you!"

Pete pulled out a monocle magnifier and held it up to his left-low eye to inspect the ports. At least two on each side looked like fluid or gas ports, and the area surrounding those looked exactly like the quick connect system used for the fuel containers on Orlin's mecha. Several other ports looked like they would have held some sort of fixture, but there was no opening in the socket to suggest either electrical or physical connection with the device.

He realized that the twins had continued talking to him as he was lost in inspecting the newly revealed features of his project.

"—so we're headed back—"

"—and we rigged—"

"—a scanner—"

"—to identify—"

"—the same components—"

"—as your suit."

Jinx—or Jerry, it was hard to tell since they were both covered in the powdered abrasive from the cleaning station—held out a device with a paw-grip and small screen. Material scanners were pretty common on Joth. They were used for everything from finding buried minerals to identifying sophont remains. He wasn't entirely sure he wanted to know where the human twins had gotten the device, but he wasn't going to turn it down.

They wouldn't have the hover sled this time, not with a missing thruster, and besides it was being refitted into something much more like the fighter profile that Jerry and Jinx had proposed for their merit badge. Instead, they'd talked their big sister Jenny into flying them over to the Rinto yard in her flitter. Pete supposed that having siblings whose names all started with "J" must be one of those family identification things, such as the "-etil" part of his own name. He didn't really understand Human naming, even though he'd grown up in the mixed-race society of Joth. Most sophonts went with whatever name their Human friends called them, especially since Humans were known for shortening names.

At least they wouldn't have to worry about Jerry and Jinx's sister sticking around to take them home from the scrap yard, either. The boys said that she was sweet on the human operating the big Grappler scrap mover at Rinto's. The problem would be convincing her to leave when they were done.

"Okay Jerx, go have fun, I'll be talking to Roland," Jenny had said when they arrived at the scrap yard. The twins immediately ran off to hunt for thrusters in a large pile of material that was new since the last time they'd visited, leaving Pete to go to the sector where they'd found the "fire-fighter suit." When he got there, he found only a patch of bare ground and a few scraps of metal. He went to find Ronnie, and earned a dirty look from Jenny in the process.

"Sorry, Pete, but that pile's been sorted. Boss said you can pick through all of the unsorted scrap, put once it's been sorted, it's in the inventory." Ronnie looked apologetic, and he probably was. He'd actually helped them load up their salvage on the first couple of trips, before the twins had assembled the hover frame.

"But, Roland, there might have been parts there for my suit! I just need to look at the stuff from that pile."

Roland looked at Pete, then at Jenny, then back at Pete again. "Okay, kid. That sector has been scanned and sorted for useable salvage, but it hasn't been category sorted, so it's still all in one place. I can let you take a look, but I gotta warn you, if it's been entered into inventory, you're going to have to buy it. I can't just let you have it or the Boss will skin me alive."

Pete tried to imagine a human with its thin dermal layer peeled open. It wasn't something he wanted to dwell on. He totally missed the wink Roland gave Jenny. He swallowed and pushed the thought out of his mind.

When Roland showed him to the container with the tagged and labeled salvage, Pete pulled out the scanner and started running it over the piled-up components that would eventually be sold to sophonts needing specific parts. None of the pieces in the collection triggered the scanner, so Pete started over, this time looking closely under and behind the stacked components, but he never saw anything that looked like it went with the suit he'd found.

There certainly were not enough items here to account for the entire volume of the pile they'd originally explored—even given the items they'd salvaged themselves. Troopmaster Zentto had ensured that few of the troop members would get into fights over the same pieces. Each patrol had been assigned different sectors, and told to stay within them at risk of being disqualified. Since it would be another two years until Maker Merit Badge came around again, it was a serious threat. So it was unlikely that another patrol had gotten to "their" salvage.

The problem was—where was everything else from the pile?

Pete hunted down Roland yet again. He'd heard that Roland had gone on break, and had last been seen on the far side of the open-sided roofed shelter where some of the larger pieces of obviously good-condition salvage were stored. He knew that Humans of Roland and Jenny's age liked to engage in what Jerry and Jinx called "snogging"—he'd certainly heard enough details of the practice from the twins—so he made sure to make a lot of noise as he approached the area where the Humans had last been seen.

Sure enough, he heard giggling and low talking from just beyond a large object that looked like a complete airlock assembly. Pete kicked a piece of debris into the airlock door, making a satisfying thunk. He waited a moment, and then Roland came around the corner, putting his eye protection and hat back on.

"Okay, pipsqueak, what do you want now?" Pete realized he was a bit small for a Human his age, but he would be nearly two meters at maturity. The scrapyard worker was probably about as tall as he would get, and would barely come up to the Caldivar's chin once he was fully grown. There was simply no need to be insulting.

"I'm sorry, Mister Roland, I really am, but... where is the rest of the scrap?" He looked around, and extended a claw to gesture with. "Each of these piles is mixed scrap. The sorted items you let me look at are only about half of the original pile. What happens to the rest?"

"Oh. Oh! Sorry kid, I guess I should have told you. If it's not sorted for labeled salvage, it gets put over there." Roland pointed to an absolutely huge pile of scrap on the far edge of the yard.

Pete's spirits fell. There was absolutely no way he was going to find anything in that pile. It was many, many times the size of the original, and looked like it had years' worth of scraps.

"Although," continued Roland, "we just finished sorting your stuff this morning. The scraps are probably still in the hopper of the Grappler..."

Pete didn't hear the rest as he took off in the direction of the bulldozer-like mecha. Roland watched him go, then muttered "whatever" and took off his hat and sunglasses and he headed back behind the airlock assembly. "Jenny, I've got another 10 minutes and then I've got to get back to work."

As soon as he reached the Grappler, he knew he'd found the right salvage. There was the burned relay and cracked power cell that Orlin and the twins had rejected on their first salvage trip. He pulled out the scanner and started to run it over the items. He was rewarded with several beeps immediately. He dug into the pile and pulled out two bottle-like objects made from the same blue-green metal as the suit. Another ten minutes yielded a total of seven items—two long bottles, two short ones, one large, <u>heavy</u> rectangular object that was exactly the size of one of the unusual sockets on the suit, and two smaller, lighter cylinders. The cylinders looked like some sort of power cell. The cylinders probably contained liquid or gas. A larger one sloshed slightly, while the smaller ones seemed to be mostly full. The heavy rectangle appeared to be solid, with no openings or obvious connections. That they went with the suit was highly probable based on the size, fittings and the unusual metal.

As for what they contained, he might have to go back to visit Breck.

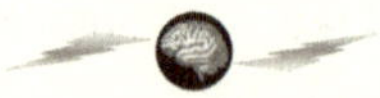

"Yes. Perfluorodecalin." Breck declared, holding up the bottle that still contained liquid. "The trace from the other bottle is the same, and they're an exact match to a variant called 'Flurodec.' The bottles are designed to hold pressurized liquid, and Flurodec is pretty dense in liquid form. It's probably a pretty good supply for fire-suppression and cooling. Are you going to want to refill them? I can synthesize some in the molecular printer. Carbon and Fluorine can be scavenged from dirt, air, water, so it will be pretty cheap. I can make a run and fill the bottles once you clean them up."

"What about the other pieces?" Pete asked.

"Well, as you said, the cylinders are power cells. They're exhausted, but it shouldn't be hard to power them up. It looks like a standard capacitor array. As for the small bottles, the pressure and weight suggests that they are probably between half and three quarters full. I can't tell what the stuff is, though; it's a complex organic mix that doesn't match anything in our database. This..." He held up the dense rectangle. "...is interesting. Its density suggests heavy metals, possibly even rare ones. The closest density match is osmium, but it's the wrong texture—this feels like a polymer, not a metal. However, I can't scan anything in the interior. It seems solid all the way through, so it's unlikely that this is just a plastic shell over heavy metal. Given the scan, this is either made up of nanometer sized or smaller components, or it's a heck of a lot better shielded than anything I've ever seen."

Breck looked at Pete expectantly.

"I'll take that refill. And thanks. Oh, by the way..." Pete reached into his coverall and pulled out Breck's watch. "Cleaned, serviced, and in a brand new case, courtesy of the Farnog student workshop."

"Wow, thanks." Breck put the watch back onto his wrist and closed the clasp. Immediately the face of the device lit up with the time and a list of the Caldivar grad student's appointments and reminders. "Yeah, no problem. I'll start the synthesizer. Bring back those bottles with the fittings cleaned up and I'll refill them for you."

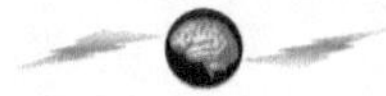

The day finally came to assemble the components of the suit and see what it did. Pete first attached each of the limb sleeves to the clamshell via the hiring and tubing harnesses. He then attached the four bottles—two large and two small—and inserted the heavy block in the matching receptacle on one side of the shell. He then attached what he assumed was the control module to the front of the clamshell. Orlin, Jerry and Jinx clustered around as he inserted the first power cell into the back of the suit.

Nothing happened.

"Are you sure—"

"—it's charged up?"

"Shut up, I charged them myself. They're not that different than the power cells for my mecha. They both registered peak charge when I tested them," answered Orlin.

"So what—"

"—do we do now?"

"Insert the other one." Orlin nodded at Pete, who felt a prickling on his long tongue, a sure sign of anxiety. It was the Caldivar equivalent of a nervous sweat.

"I <choo> want <choo> to do <choo> a test <choo> first," Pete said. He had sneezed a couple of times since arriving at the workshop; now it seemed as if he couldn't stop. He'd felt the first signs of a respiratory infection the night before, but he'd hoped the medicine he'd taken that morning would suffice until they finished the day's testing. There was only one more week to complete the project and register it for the Maker Faire. He needed to test it today.

"Are you okay, Pete?"

Pete stared back at Jerry, dumbfounded. It was the first time in his experience that one of the twins had spoken a complete sentence on his own. Jinx looked on with a concerned expression. "It's okay, 'just a head cold' I think you'd call it."

"Sounds like more of a 'nose cold,' Jinx corrected. Pete was used to his friends teasing him about his long flexible snout, but Jinx seemed genuinely concerned. "That has got—"

"—to hurt," finished Jerry.

The surreal moment had passed. The twins were back to splitting sentences. "I'll be okay. Let me run this test, then plug in the other power cell."

He had a multiband spectral analyzer plugged into his slate. A check of the suit showed no activity. After pausing to sneeze a couple more times, he plugged in the second power cell. Again, the scanner showed no activity.

"It doesn't work," Pete muttered.

"Wait—"

"—look at this."

Jerry pointed to the odd rectangular block. A seam appeared in the otherwise solid block and was lit by a faint orange light. Meanwhile, the rectangular socket on the other side of the clamshell was pulsing with the same orange light. Jinx reached out to touch the block and it came apart at the seam.

"Maybe you should—"

"—plug this in—"

"—over there?"

Jinx handed the half block to Pete, who looked it over carefully. It was just like the original block, only half the size. There was no evidence it had ever been part of a larger object, yet strangely, it felt just as heavy as the original. He shrugged. "Might as well."

Once the block was plugged into the open socket, the light stopped pulsing, and a brief flicker showed on the screen of the control module. The multi-band scanner showed that there was some electronic activity in the control module, and a faint electromagnetic field emanating from torso of the suit.

Aside from that, there was no other indication or response from the suit.

"You have to—"

"—put it on."

"Yes, Pete." Orlin nodded concurrence with the twins. "This is the last part. You have to put it on to see how it works. You've done all of this work re-assembling and restoring it. Don't you want to see how it works?"

"To be honest, <choo> I been waiting <choo> to see what it does on its own, first." As soon as Pete got the last words out, he started a sneezing fit that lasted for almost a minute.

"Are you sure you're okay?" Orlin looked at him with concern, but then his expression turned into a smirk. "Or is this just an excuse to back out?"

"No balls," whispered Jinx.

"No balls." Jerry repeated the taunt with a bit more volume.

"Eff you, Lizard Face!" Pete managed between sneezes. "And you too, Monkey Twins!"

The sneezing and now the taunting were giving Pete a splitting headache. With a glare, he stomped over to the bench set up at the foot of the assembly table. The suit was attached to a rack that would lift it upright off of the table and over the bench, so that he could sit and just pull the clamshell down over his torso. It was too big around and too tall for him, but his hips were still slim enough at his age that the suit would settle over his shoulders and just hang halfway to his knees.

It was almost anticlimactic.

Almost.

The one unexpected occurrence was that as the clamshell slid down over his body, the surface separated into plates and readjusted to perfectly fit him. Then it just seemed to sit there.

Jinx ran the scanner over him while Jerry took a bunch of pictures with his slate. Orlin had been taking a continuous video recording, but the Human used a close-up setting to capture the details of the now-perfectly-adjusted suit.

"That's a whole lot of nothing," complained Pete.

"Yes, but now—"

"—your suit fits."

"You probably have to put the sleeves on." Orlin handed Pete the first of the four tubes, which now seemed to be sized exactly right for Pete.

Even with the full suit on, it didn't seem to do anything. On the other paw, it was now obvious that their earlier surmise that the suit would leave the hips and shoulders unprotected was incorrect. The torso appeared to have pauldrons to cover the shoulders right up to the top of the sleeves. The torso also extended over the groin and buttocks while the legs extended from ankles all the way over the pelvis and hip bones. The comparison with armor was apt, given that it seemed to cover everything except head, paws and feet, but it wasn't actually protecting him. They'd already determined that the fabric couldn't be cut by anything in their shop, but when Pete challenged Jinx to hit him in the stomach, the suit did absolutely nothing to block or lessen the blow.

That <u>hurt</u>!

At least, it hurt briefly. There was a slight flash of the chest display, but nothing else aside from a single green light at the top of the panel.

The suit was also hot. Caldivar didn't sweat like Humans, but he did start to pant from increased body temperature. Yet, almost as soon as he started, the suit seemed to cool off.

"It's cooling."

"Maybe it goes—"

"—under a spacesuit?"

"Whatever it is, it needs to wait until tomorrow," Pete said. "I've been feeling bad all day, and now I'm pretty tired. I just want to go home and sleep."

"Go ahead. We're headed out to Beggar's Canyon to field test Stomper and Zoomer tomorrow." Orlin used the names that Jerry and Jinx had applied to the mecha and two-seat flyer, respectively.

"Thanks." Pete sat back down on the bench and started pulling off the sleeves. He hung them on the rack, and almost before he could reach for the catches on the clamshell, it shifted back to the original, oversized configuration. Jinx hooked the storage rack to a loop just inside the collar of the torso while Jerry released a weighted arm that lifted the suit right off of the young Caldivar.

"Hey, did you—"

"—see that?"

"Some words—"

"—on the panel."

Pete turned to Orlin. "Did you get that on the video?" When his friend nodded, he continued, "Zip that over to my slate. I'll try to look at it later." The headache was receding, and it felt like he'd be able to manage not sneezing for a while, so he'd try to look at the video of the test when he got home. In fact, he wasn't feeling quite as tired, but he wasn't sure why.

As one last step for the evening, he and his friends removed the bottles and power cells from the suit. The rectangular blocks, however, did not want to come loose. In fact, it wasn't possible to detect the seams at the edges of the sockets. It was strange that the block had divided in tow, and now couldn't be removed—almost as if the suit had decided that those sockets needed to be filled and stay that way.

He'd worry about that tomorrow.

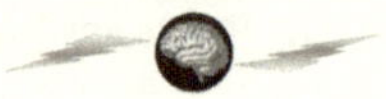

"Have you ever seen this script before?"

Cousin Breck was studying for his comprehensive exams, and made it clear that he was not to be disturbed, so Pete took the video still images to Troop-master Zentto. The adult troop leader didn't recognize the symbols that had appeared on the control module of the suit, so he had referred the scout to an older human professor at Tretrayon Academy.

"It's an older machine script known as 'Roman,'" said Professor Gannon. "One of the variants of Earth Common from a few thousand years ago. Every once in a while we'll make contact with one of the Lost Colonies and their systems will use Roman. I have a book here somewhere."

The professor's office had something that Pete had never seen before—real, physical books. There were floor-to-ceiling shelves filled with the rectangular objects of various heights, lengths and widths. The professor carefully stood up from his desk and slowly moved to select one such book from a shelf. He laid it open on the desk and opened it to show the symbols printed on the individual pages. Unlike the classical books sometimes shown in old vid'tainment, these weren't actually made from the cellulose pulp that used to be known as "paper," but rather from a thin polymer not unlike the screen of a slate. The images weren't all static, either. Several pages contained searchable indices, and optical fibers displaying colored prompts helped identify locations with the book where searched text could be found.

The book was remarkable, but he hoped that the professor wasn't expecting him to take it and perform a translation by paw. The thought must have shown on his face, because Professor Gannon laughed and reached into a drawer, pulling out a long, thin cylinder, about one-half centime by eighteen centimeters. He tapped one end to the binding of the book, and both binding and cylinder pulsed green for a moment. He then took the cylinder, grabbed it in the middle, separating it lengthwise, revealing a thin membrane stretched between the two half-cylinders. The membrane was approximately the dimensions of as slate screen, and sure enough, the membrane adhered to the screen when placed over it.

"That's a translation filter. I programmed it with the Roman symbology. It will translate the symbols for you, and may even be able to interpret some of the words, but I must caution you." Gannon looked at Pete sternly, and lifted one eyebrow. "It may not be a dialect of Common that you are familiar with. If these symbols come from a Lost World Artifact, there's no telling how much the language has drifted. Good luck, son."

Pete thanked him and headed back home from the university. He was tempted to visit Breck just to see how he was doing, but he got a "Do Not Disturb" response when he tried to text his cousin. Well then, he'd just have to inform Breck of his results on another day.

Once back in the workshop, Pete started to work on the translation. In all, Orlin had captured five different video sequences where symbols appeared on the screen of the control module. Pete had begged off on the testing today, and his patrol-mates had headed off to the canyon on their own. They still had five more days, so Pete was going to get this translation done this afternoon while his friends were out.

The professor was correct, the translator overlay converted the symbols, but the words were unfamiliar. They seemed as if he should know them, however, and a couple of hours on the 'net searching thousand years-old Earth Common dialects gave him some rough translations.

The first text had appeared when the rectangular block had split. The translation didn't make a lot of sense:

Nanite source unbalanced.

The next sequence occurred when the clamshell resized itself to his body:

Biomorphic adjustment, species 1732, juvenile.

The third message was quite a bit longer, and appeared soon after he'd finished pulling on all of the sleeves:

Allergen detected.

Imidazole-ethanamine levels elevated.

Eicosanoid PgI levels elevated.

Administer antihistamine and cyclooxygenase inhibitor.

He didn't know all of the words, but Pete knew that some of them were medical terms. The fourth message was more of the same:

Blunt impact trauma. Tissue damage. Organ bruising.

Administer hematoma nanites 1732.42.

Temperature imbalance. Cooling.

The final message put it all in perspective:

Treatment complete.

If Pete was interpreting these messages correctly, he had actually been seriously hurt when he had Jinx punch him in the stomach. The suit had treated the injury, and all he'd felt was a brief pain from the impact. A few more minutes on the 'net revealed that he'd been in the middle of an allergy attack when he'd first donned the suit. It diagnosed and treated his sneezes and headache.

No wonder he'd felt better by the time he finished testing that day.

He still wasn't sure what was meant by "nanite source unbalanced" but apparently both sockets needed to be filled with the dense material, so maybe that was the nanite source. As for "species 1732" that was likely a reference to being a Caldivar. After all, he <u>was</u> a juvenile and hadn't reached his full adult height yet.

With this new knowledge, Pete decided to put the power cells back in and don the suit to see if he could get any other responses. Sure, he was healthy now, but the only time he'd really gotten a response was when he was wearing it.

He propped his slate up on the workbench where he could see it, and detached the video pickup so that he could place it in position to view the chest readouts. He then sat on the bench and pulled the clamshell down over his head. Once again it configured himself to his body, and he saw "Biomorphic adjustment, species 1732, juvenile," followed by a new message that read: "Health check complete, no treatment needed."

Okay, so he was healthy. Now he needed to see if he could get any other response. After about an hour of trying to get a response from the control module—and succeeding to a limited extent—he translated a message that read:

Enhanced Medical Technician Operator Interface (Y/N)?

Pete figured there was nothing to lose, so he tapped on the symbol that was being translated as the letter "Y" in Earth Common. Almost immediately he noticed a prickling sensation in his paws and that his vision was sharper. He looked closely at the mottled gray skin of his paws, and noticed a very fine network of fibers, terminating in what looked like sensor pads on the tips of his digits. Looking in the video playback from this slate camera, he noticed a similar network on his cheeks, and leading up to his lower two eyes. When he touched the skin of his face to see what the fibers were, he immediately began to see a readout of skin temperature, moisture content, hydration, pulse, respiration rate, and other body conditions. The test showed up directly in his vision.

More surprisingly, it was in Caldivar Upper, the technical language of his people. All Caldivar learned to read Caldi-Up at the same time they learned Earth Common. Even if their particular community mostly most Caldi-Low, Caldi-Up was used for all scientific, technical and engineering communication. If you were educated, you knew Caldi-Up. He supposed he shouldn't be surprised. This had to be another feature of the Suit. It knew he was Caldivar, thus it was communicating in the appropriate language.

He noticed that it was getting dark. Orlin and the twins weren't back yet. He wondered why they were out so long. It would have long since been dark down in the canyon by now, and if they had left when the light failed, they should be back by now.

He no sooner had the thought than he heard the whine of an approaching flyer. It _sounded_ like the thrusters the twins had mounted in Zoomer, but it also sounded like they were unbalanced. There was a vibration that he could almost feel, and one of the thrusters seemed to be sputtering as if it had an uneven fuel feed. He stepped outside to greet his friends and find out what had happened to the flyer, and was shocked at the appearance of a badly damaged vehicle with only one occupant. One of the twins was in the cockpit, and from the appearance, he was having difficulty controlling the vehicle.

"Jerry? Or Jinx? What happened?"

The Human, Jinx—as evidenced by a small scar on his chin, the only distinguishing feature between the two—was smeared in blood and was holding his left arm close to his body. It didn't look right, and Pete noticed a new set of symbols appearing in his vision. He didn't have time to pay attention to those just yet, as he tried to pay attention to what Jinx was saying.

"Pete come quick—" He paused, as if waiting for his twin to finish the sentence. He gulped as he realized that he was alone for one of the few times in his life. "Jerry's hurt, but Orlin's hurt <u>bad</u>. Stomper crashed into Zoomer and we both hit the canyon wall." We need your help to get Orlin out of his mecha so we can get him to medical help."

Pete took in the information, and then noticed the text flashing in his lower right vision:

Probable osteo fracture. Contact diagnostics needed.

"Hold on, Jinx, let me help you." Jinx was trying to slide out of the pilot position. He winced every time he had to move his left arm. Pete touched him on the shoulder and was rewarded with more diagnostic information:

Compound fracture, left radius, simple fracture, left ulna.
Subcutaneous hematoma. No internal injuries.

He felt his left sleeve begin to loosen, and then it split lengthwise down the middle.

Limb component L1 configured for independent operation.
Place splint on injured limb and activate.
Continue? (Y/N).

He tried to concentrate on the text in his vision. How was he supposed to respond to something projected directly at his eyes? There was no physical symbol to touch or tap?

The sleeve was threatening to fall off, so he grabbed at it with his right paw. The fabric, tubing, wires and all, easily came loose from the clamshell. The ports in the edge of the carapace appeared to have come with it, since the connections terminated in a small rectangular block similar to the "nanite source" blocks.

That must be the "independent operation" part. He carefully placed it over Jinx's left arm and attempted to seal it. It appeared to have dilated to even larger than its resting state, so Pete just settled for overlapping the two edges. It must have been enough, because the moment he did so, the sleeve tightened and the embedded tubing became rigid, forming a hard splint to realign and support the broken bone.

Jinx gave out a quick "Agh!" of pain as the sleeve stiffened, then a relaxed sigh. Pete saw:

Fracture immobilized.

and:

Analgesic administered.

in his vision.

"Okay, let's get moving." Pete climbed into the pilot station of the flyer. Yeah, it was rough, but he'd assisted the twins with the assembly—they'd each helped each other with the projects—so he should be able to fly it out to the canyon. "Beggar's Canyon, right? Where in the canyon?"

"Down by the thermal ports."

It was a region of turbulent winds, fueled by geothermal vents that vented hot gases into an already narrow stretch of canyon.

"What the hell were you fools doing down there? You were supposed to stay up near the moisture extractors!"

"Everything was going so well, we decided to step up the testing to the next level. Stomper was so stable and Zoomer so responsive that we thought that a little bit of wind wouldn't hurt."

Pete just shook his head.

During the twenty-minute flight out to the canyon, Jinx continued to talk about the testing, never once mentioning—or noticing—that Pete was wearing the suit and one arm was currently serving as a cast on the Human's arm.

Pete just thought about what he would do… what he <u>could</u> do… once they were at the canyon. He'd brought his slate. In fact, as he had been trying to figure out where to carry it, a pocket opened up on the front of the clamshell. Before leaving the workshop, he'd triggered the emergency locator beacon on the slate, sending it to his parents, Troopmaster Zentto, and Cousin Breck. He'd used a code that indicated that he, personally, was okay, but that he needed assistance. The adults could track his slate to find them. Hopefully they could get there before it was too late.

When they reached Beggar's Canyon, Pete set the flyer down a cautious distance from the Thermal Ports and walked the rest of the way with Jinx. They found the wrecked mecha with Jerry sitting beside it. Orlin's face was barely visible through the open visor of the combat armor. His face was very pale, the normally blue-green scales tinged with gray, and his eyes were closed. Jerry was pale as well. He tried to stand when the pair approached, but his right leg wouldn't support his weight.

A red circle appeared in Pete's vision superimposed over Jerry's knee, but it was when he looked at what he could see of Orlin that the display was filled with alerts and flashing indicators. Since he already had an inkling of the suit's response, he stepped up to Jerry and placed a paw over his knee.

Ruptured right anterior cruciate ligament.

The right leg sleeve loosened, and as he had anticipated, his visual display said:

Limb component R2 configured for independent operation.
Place splint on injured limb and activate.
Continue? (Y/N).

It occurred to him that he still didn't know how he was supposed to respond to the query. On Jinx, he'd simply put the sleeve on the injured limb and the suit did the rest.

Once again, he removed the expanded sleeve. He wrapped it around Jerry's leg, but this time he was able to mate the edges together. The sleeve sealed itself up and inflated. He saw the confirmation message and the information that medication had been delivered.

Now for Orlin. One of the arms of the mecha had come loose at the shoulder joint. Pete and the now-mobile Jerry carefully removed the mechatronic limb, exposing the Prithmar's scaly skin.

Pete touched Orlin's arm, and the display started scrolling a large amount of information. It stopped and then flashed an instruction to remove the right arm sleeve and apply it to his badly injured patrol-mate. This time he noticed that the fittings for the large and small bottles on that side also came loose from the clamshell when he pulled off the sleeve. Once the sleeve was on Orlin, his vision displayed several long messages. Each paused in his vision just long enough for him to see and understand it before the next message appeared.

> *Severe trauma and shock.*
> *Concussion.*
> *Multiple internal injuries.*
> *Internal bleeding.*
> *Multiple compound fractures.*
> *Blood pressure low, administering Flurodec volume expander.*
> *WARNING: Leak in FLURODEC reservoir.*
> *Leak is within tolerable limits. Continue? (Y/N)*

There was a vaguely sweet smell in the air, and he could hear a slight hissing. It was the fluorocarbon tank. There must have been a hidden crack. He concentrated on the Yes/No query, and saw the Y flash green. The readout continued:

> *Multiple internal injuries.*
> *Medical stasis required. Trauma nanites required.*
> *Remove central somatic unit and place on patient.*
> *Continue? (Y/N)*

Central somatic? Oh. Soma meant body. He needed to put the clamshell on Orlin, but they needed to get him out of the damaged mecha first. He concentrated on N and saw it flash ready. The question remained in his vision.

"We have to get him out of there. Jerry? Jinx? How do we get him out?"

"There's an emergency eject—"

"—under his chin. But I didn't want to do that before help got here. I think a piece of the hatch is sticking into him. I didn't want to him to start bleeding when I pulled it out."

Pete looked at jerry, surprised at the long speech without his twin's interruption.

"You mean 'start bleeding more...'" Jinx added.

Jerry looked down at the blood on his shirt, pants, and on the front of the mecha.

"Well, we have to get him out. I can't say for certain that he won't start bleeding some more, but the only way to treat him is to get him out of there, and get this," Pete rapped his knuckles on the chest plate of the suit "onto him."

No sooner had he uttered the words, than his display signaled:

Patient stability limited. Current blood loss within acceptable limits.

Place central somatic unit on patient within the next fifteen minutes.

Additional Flurodec blood substitute being administered to compensate for removal of primary impalement.

Proceed with patient extraction.

The last sentence wasn't a question. It was a command.

"Okay, guys, let's pop the lid. Once it's open, you lift him out and I'll slip the clamshell over him." The moment he said it, the catches on the torso of the suit popped open, and the plates rearranged into a larger volume to accommodate their injured friend.

There was indeed a projection of the suit hatch penetrating Orlin's body. The moment the cover came open, there was a spurt of blood, and the hissing sound increased.

Pete pulled the clamshell over his head and was surprised to see that a small ring of suit material remained around his neck, connected to the network of fibers on his paws and face.

Okay, I guess that's how he would continue to control the suit.

The three youth managed to get Orlin free enough from the mecha to get the clamshell over his upper body. Once lowered over his form, it configured itself to whatever parts of the Prithmar's body that it could contact. A continuous stream of diagnostics and treatments scrolled through Pete's vision and stopped with one final message:

Trauma Nanites type 2460.9 administered.

Medical stasis achieved. Transport patient to medical facility.

EMT Mk XI service required at conclusion of independent operation.

The text blinked for a minute, and then was replaced by a graphical readout of Orlin's pulse and respiration rate, blood pressure, body temperature, and oxygen saturation rate. A new displayed appeared in his upper eye, depicting a map of the region with a flashing icon moving toward the canyon. Pete knew that somehow, the suit had interfaced with his slate and was tracking the adults racing to their position.

Now that all three boys were treated, and help was on the way, Pete stopped to look around at the crash site.

It was completely dark.

It had been maybe an hour since Jinx had arrived at the workshop—dusk up on the plains, but well into night down here in the canyon. It would have been completely dark even before they arrived, but he'd been able to see perfectly throughout the whole rescue. Caldivar had good night vision, after all, they were a burrowing species, but it didn't explain the fact that the only reason he knew it was dark was because of the color of the sky.

His own vision might have been a result of the suit's optical fibers enhancing his vision, but what about Jerry and Jinx? They seemed to be able to see pretty well, too.

"Now that your body—"

"—isn't glowing like daylight—"

"—can we turn on a light?"

Zerith Farnog had returned to Joth as a special guest presenter for the Joth Maker Faire. The Prithmar was one of Salvage System President Tomeral's closest friends, and had been an important part of construction and innovation that had helped President Tomeral defeat first the Squilla threatening Tretra and Joth, then the Squilla home world (not to mention the Krith and the Gritloth). He was one of the principal shareholders of Tomeral and Associates, and shared the company's reputation for hating bullies, but supporting sophonts struggling to be self-reliant. It had once been rumored that he was responsible for establishing the Maker Faire, but it was just that, a rumor. On the other paw, his parent's company, Farnog Corp, was one of the main sponsors for the youth category.

Zerith had to stand on a platform to be able to place the Special Award medallion over Pete's head. Troopmaster Zentto had already pinned on his Maker Merit Badge and his new Senior Class rank insignia, as well as recognition for lifesaving. Now it was time for the <u>big</u> moment.

"Pettekil Emil. It is my pleasure to award you this Special Award for your discovery, restoration and most importantly, analysis of the Trauma Suit. While Maker Faire awards are generally for sophonts who make their entries from components, the Maker Faire Council has decided that your work in restoring the Emergency Medical Technician Mark XI support garment is worth recognition. The last of these suits was thought lost more than two thousand years ago. To find one and recognize what it was—not to mention restoring it to working order <u>before</u> you knew what it was—is a remarkable achievement. Thanks to your work, we not only have a working suit, but also the information we need to duplicate it.

"For that, Joth, Tretra, Farnog Corp and Tomeral and Associates thank you."

The audience started to applaud, and Pete felt a flush of embarrassment. He suppressed the urge to sneeze. There was no point in starting that again, although...

About thirty seconds in The Suit would take care of it.

CHEATING THE ODDS

Authors note: When Kevin Steverson gave me the chance to write again for his universe, of course I had to continue the tales of Pete, Orlin, Jerry, and Jinx.

"This-s is most definitely *not* my idea of camping. It'ss too wet, it'ss too cool, it'ss too... foresssty." Orlin was complaining, pretty much the same as he had ever since the drop pods had deposited them in Tretra's equatorial jungle. "I thought s-survival training was done in deserts-s? I can *handle* deserts-s."

"Actually, that's why survival training for Joth natives is conducted on Tretra," replied Pete. "Tretra natives complete the Extreme Environment Survival Exercise—EESE School on Joth, we do it on Tretra. The whole *point* is to push us to an environment we are adapted to."

"Besides it's not—," began Jerry.

"—supposed to be just 'camping,'" finished Jinx.

Jerry and Jinx were human twins, and had a very bad habit of finishing each other's sentences. It was enough to give a sophont whiplash. They were also the youngest of the quartet.

Orlin was a Prithmar, lizardlike, and technically the oldest of the group, but his kind didn't count the year spent as an undeveloped newt, before their neural ganglia differentiated into their species' equivalent of a brain. As it was, he realistically edged out the twins by about six months in developmental age, even as they held the height advantage.

Pete—only his mother called him Pettekil—was a Caldivar, anteater like with a long flexible nose and three eyes. He was also older than the twins by more than a year, and older than Orlin by two months, as long as one didn't count the latter's year as a newt. For that sin, and one other, he had been named Squad Leader for this exercise.

The "other sin" occurred just under two years ago when he had been working on Maker Merit Badge, discovered an odd protective suit in a salvage yard and reconditioned it. Thinking it to be a protective garment for firefighters, he had been surprised to discover that it was a product of a Lost Technology—an emergency medical technician's field wearable aid kit. For his ingenuity and level-headedness in rescuing his companions when all three were injured testing their own Maker Badge refurbishments, Pete had been awarded many honors, including a guaranteed place in The Academy run by Tomeral and Associates. After graduation next year, he would train with the Tretrayon military for two years, then transfer to Salvage System for the rest of his study. Pete had a guaranteed spot, but Orlin, Jerry and Jinx still had to earn their own—but with a considerable boost from their own Maker projects as well as their roles in helping Pete with the EMT suit.

The past two years had been uncertain, but as of the end of the most recent school year, they'd learned that all four would be heading to The Academy on graduation. Thus, they had to spend the summer preparing for the physical challenges of Salvage System's unique service, and one of those preparations was Survival School. Pete's seniority both by developmental age and his in-coming-cadet ranking put him in charge of their cadet squad for this training exercise.

Most of the Tretrayon Academy cadets did their survival far from the urban and temperate climate of home, in other words, on Tretra's sister world of Joth. However, those who grew up in the sparsely-populated hot, arid deserts of Joth were sent to the forests and jungles of Tretra to learn emergency survival skills;

hence why Pete and his squad found themselves in a high-elevation cloud-forest, dealing with chilling wet conditions and unable to see much of the sky or horizon.

"I'm cold," said Jerry and Jinx simultaneously, for once not speaking in tag-term fashion.

Pete checked his wrist-comp. "Well, we're at twenty-four hundred meters elevation. We might be pretty much *on* the equator, but the altitude means it's going to get chilly tonight. Let's go ahead and make camp, it will be night in about an hour. The instructors said we should always make camp when there was enough light for not just pitching shelters, but also for anything else we need to do afterward.

The "need to do afterward" meant trying to fix a meal, and that meant trying to find something to eat. All four of the "boys" could eat fruit, nuts and berries. Prithmar were largely vegetarian, and like many of his race, Orlin was constantly snacking on a particularly crunchy or juicy fruit or vegetable at home. He'd been grumbling about the lack of snacks for the past day. Jerry and Jinx were omnivores, and it had been said that humans would eat anything that wasn't tied down. As a Caldivar, Pete was also an omnivore, but a little fussier about where his protein came from. At home they had Tretrayon vat-meat, as well as domesticated herds of small Joth desert animals and cool-house-raised agriculture. When traveling, there were always full-calorie meal bars. The Tretrayon version were pretty bland, but the new ones coming from Salvage System were said to be nutritious *and* delicious.

Unfortunately, this was a survival exercise and none of that was available. They had water purification systems and electrolyte tablets, vitamins suitable for several species, and had been allowed one supplement. Naturally, Orlin had chosen Joobla Oil for his supplement. The incredibly spicy oil was much too strong for Pete and the twins, but Orlin said it made most food "just barely palatable." Pete had opted for a concentrated protein paste. He and Orlin gathered local fruits, nuts and berries. That would save his delicate stomach the indignity of eating grilled forest rodent—or worse, raw forest rodent—for a few more days. Jinx and Jerry had packed something called "curry" and were currently cooking a fragrant stew from scavenged roots and the meat of an arboreal rodent with a large bushy tail.

After they cleaned up the remnants of their meal, Orlin snuggled into his insulating thermal shelter. The exothermic Joth native was at a distinct disadvantage in this environment. Jerry and Jinx should have fared much better, humans had adapted to every environment, as long as they had breathable air. Unfortunately, the best way to described the twins was "spoiled." They'd lived on hot, arid Joth all of their lives, and were shivering even in their heavy garments. It surprised Pete that of the quartet, he felt the least discomfort, even though the air was much wetter than his race's desert home-world. Dry air produced extreme temperature swings, so the cold wasn't an issue, just the humidity, and even that could be handled with the appropriate clothing.

It might be a survival experience, but it was a challenge, and Pete was in his element.

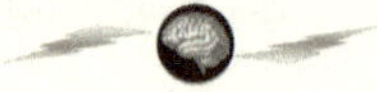

The early morning sun filtered through the trees and started a chorus of chirps, trills, squeaks and caws. Orlin was still in the warm embrace of his shelter. Pete could hear him snoring. Jerry and Jinx were moving around in their tent, the mosquito netting at the entrance still firmly closed, so they were probably applying insect repellant. Orlin and Pete didn't need it, none of the Tretrayon insects could penetrate the Prithmar's scales or the Caldivar's tough skin.

Pete had chosen to hang a hammock from two sturdy trees. The airflow above and below his nesting place had helped keep the humidity tolerable, and it also helped him keep an eye on the rest of "his" squad. He looked up and saw motion in the tops of the trees—birds from the sound. There was a slight rustling sound off to the south. That was likely another of the arboreals like the one Jerry and Jinx cooked last night.

Speaking of which...

"Uh, my stomach—"

"—doesn't feel right."

The boys quickly unzipped and raced out of their tent to the bushes over where they'd dug the hygiene trench the night before. The sound of retching was quickly replaced with groans, and then with argument.

"I told you to cook the *skwirl* some more."

"—and I told you it was too tough and stringy. Well done would have been impossible to chew."

"Not if it makes us sick!"

"It wasn't the *skwirl*, it was the *mushrunes*. I warned you they were poisonous."

"It wasn't the *mushrunes*, but those *toobers* were questionable..."

"Actually, I think you both ate too much." Pete climbed down from his perch, his long nose wrinkling at the smell from the hygiene area. "Now I know why your sister always refers to you by a single name... 'Jerx.' You're both acting like it. Besides, you used so much curry powder, there's no way anything could have survived. In fact, I can still smell it." He held up a paw and pinched the end of his long, anteater-like proboscis.

Jerry turned to look, and his skin paled. He turned for the hygiene trench and retched again, soon followed by Jinx.

"We can't have you two doing that. You'll be weak and dehydrated before we get to the extraction point. It's only two more nights and fifteen kilometers, but you're not going to be able to make it this way.

"If only you had—"

"—your EMT suit!"

"Y-You kn-know th-they'd n-never h-have l-let h-him k-keep it," came a new voice, teeth chattering in the cold morning air.

"Well, good morning, Orlin. Did you sleep well?"

"F-F-Fargle y-you, P-Pete, I w-was n-nice and w-warm in there, but I couldn't s-stand listening to Jerx-ss argue!" Orlin's shivering seemed to calm down, but his species' characteristic lisp came back in its absence.

"You're right, the suit is at Farnog Corp, back on Joth." He started rummaging in his pack, and pulled out a pair of heavy gloves custom designed for Caldivar paws. "But everyone brought their own pair of gloves, right?" He held up a pair of gloves made of a dull gray fabric. The cuffs were wide and thicker than the opening of the cuff. He put them on and they shrank to fit. A fine thread of silver extended from each glove, climbed his arm and joined just at the base of his neck. Another thread climbed from the junction up to the side of Pete's head and formed a small cluster at the base of his lower right eye.

"Ooh, me first!" said Jerry. "I'm sickest."

"No, me," responded Jinx.

Pete turned his third eye, the uppermost one, toward Orlin and rolled it. It was a talent he had perfected over the years of friendship with the human twins.

"How about two at a time?" Pete placed one gloved paw on the arm of each of the boys. "Ooh, it's not the *skwirl* or the *mushrunes*. You've got a water-based bacterium. Were you drinking water straight out of the stream?"

"Well, sure—"

"—it's so clean—"

"—we didn't think—"

"—it would be a problem."

"You didn't think. Why did we expect anything less of you, *Jerx*?" interrupted Orlin.

"I wouldn't talk," Pete addressed the Prithmar. "You've got scale-rot at the base of your neck. Did you use your antifungal spray last night?"

"No" Orlin looked about as sheepish as a six-foot tall lizard could manage.

"Well, let me get everyone fixed up so that we can finish packing camp and get moving to the extraction zone."

"Isn't that cheating?" Orlin pointed to the gloves.

"Well, we're expected to carry a first-aid kit, and before we do the advanced EESE school on Salvage, we'll be trained in a lot more sophisticated treatment. Besides, they're talking about deploying EMT Mark XIs with all Salvage teams before we even *get* to the Academy. I understand the Bolts will even have a version with fluorescent blue lightning all over it."

"Good. Me first then—"

"—no, me—"

The twins went back to arguing. Pete motioned to Orlin. "Let's treat that scale fungus, okay?"

By mid-day they had descended almost a thousand meters, and the temperatures were rising quite a bit. They were approaching a small river that they were supposed to ford, then ascend another five hundred meters to their evening camp near the summit of a ridge separating the outback region from their extraction point. The final day would have them descend almost two-thousand meters to the edge of the equatorial plain. Temperatures by that point would be approaching that of some of the cooler regions of Joth, but with nearly one-hundred percent humidity. Dehydration would be one of their major concerns, along with the possibility of falls and twisted ankles from the rapid descent. They had one more night at high elevation, and then one nearly at sea level.

After sun-up on the third day, they could safely activate their emergency locator beacon without washing out of the course. If they were within two kilometers of the base camp when they activated the beacon, they'd be given directions to the extraction point via the two-way radio in the beacon. That would earn them the maximum points for the course. If they were further away when the beacon was activated, extraction could come to them, but they'd lose points. If they encountered a true emergency at any time, the beacon would summon rescue, but whether they failed out or had to repeat would be determined by a review of the emergency itself. Pete was determined that his squad would earn the highest possible score for this exercise, and kept the beacon locked away in its protective box. He knew it tracked and monitored them anyway, but he wasn't about to risk accidently triggering it before the appropriate time.

Which made it oh, so difficult when Jerry almost fell over the injured man.

He was human, middle aged, so he wasn't one of the EESE students. He was lying near the edge of a small stream that joined the river about twenty meters from their chosen crossing point. He was unconscious, most likely due to the large discolored bruise on his left temple, and had bled a fair amount from a scalp wound just above his left ear.

"Do you think—"

"—he's an examiner?" asked Jerry and Jinx.

"He's-ss too old to be a s-student, and not in an EESE-ss insstructor uniform," Orlin replied, coming over to investigate.

"He seems to have fallen here. There's blood on this rock." Pete pointed to a red and brown-stained rock the size of two human fists. He poked at it with the stick he'd been using to steady himself during the morning's descent. "He didn't fall on it, though. There's blood on the underside."

"...Unless-ss it fell with him," supplied Orlin.

"Or that. Hmm." Pete bent and examined the man with all three eyes. "He's breathing a bit slow, and there's no sign of other injuries of broken bones. He's not lying in a position that suggests he was moved, though. There's not much disturbed vegetation, so he hasn't moved on his own since this happened." He reached over and touched the scalp laceration, and peered closely with his upper eye, the one with greater acuity. "He's been here long enough that the insects have gotten into the wound."

"S-so get out your magic gloves-ss and fix him."

"But what if—"

"—this is a test?"

"Maybe, but this might also be too much for just the gloves. After all, it took half of the suit to stabilize you," Pete looked pointedly at Orlin.

"True, but I had internal injuries-ss, too."

"Point." Pete crouched down and pressed a paw to the man's neck to check the man's pulse. It was slow and weak. He touched the skin of the man's cheek, and there was no twitch. He tapped his fingers in the inside of the elbow and saw a faint muscle twitch. He then took hold of one hand, extended one of his claws and pressed down right in the center of a fingernail. He held it long enough to watch the skin turn white, then released the pressure and counted how long it took for the skin to turn pink again.

As the other three boys watched in amazement, Pete switched sides and repeated the tests with the other arm and hand, and then again with both legs. Instead of taking the man's boots off, he did the pressure test on the side of the leg just above the boot-top.

"Where did you learn—"

"—to do that?"

"You've been s-studying."

Ever since Pete had found the EMT suit, he'd gotten interested in medicine. His cousin Breck was a graduate student and had helped him with the materials for the suit. After they'd been recognized for the restoration job on the rare medical mecha, Breck had also introduced his younger cousin to several of the professors, many of whom had asked about future educational plans. Despite still being in high school, he'd wondered aloud about studying and becoming a flight surgeon. That had led to more introductions, and some "extracurricular" lessons and reading assignments. He still wasn't sure if that's what he wanted to do after The Academy, but he'd learned a lot over the past two years.

"Okay, his breathing and heart rate are slow and faint, but steady. Reflexes are good, so it's unlikely he has a neck or back injury. Reperfusion is delayed, so his blood pressure is low. He's certainly not faking it."

Pete took off his pack and reached for the gloves. In doing so, he touched the housing with the emergency beacon. He could activate the transmitter and call in a rescue for the injured man. He supposed he could ask the rescue party to allow his squad to continue and finish the exercise, but he wasn't sure if they'd be allowed.

Let's just see what the diagnostics say, first.

The familiar display formed in front of his right-side, lower eye. There was a flashing yellow message instructing him to touch one glove to the injured man for more complete diagnostics. He blinked and shifted his focus several times to dismiss several "helpful" offers to put an alert on the EMT network to call in assistance. Pete had to likewise cancel queries for retrieving additional EMT Mark XI components, and to refer the patient for immediate medical assistance.

Finally, he convinced the limited artificial intelligence of the gloves to list the standard, unassisted first aid that they could administer on their own. The nanite reservoir in the cuffs of the gloves was severely limited, and all that could be administered was a pain reliever and a drug to maintain blood pressure. If and when the man woke up, they would have to get him to eat and drink to restore his strength.

Now, how were they going to get him out of here?

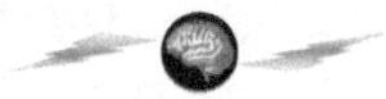

"It's called a TRA-viss—"

"—no, a tra-VOYSE!"

"Technically, it is-ss a tra-VWAH."

"Guys, I know what a travois is." Pete held up a paw to stop the argument. "However, I don't think that bumping this man along a mountain trail is going to be good for his injuries."

"So, we pull it on the smooth dirt trails—" began Jerry.

"—and carry both end over the rocks," finished Jinx

"Oh. Okay, that makes more sense."

"Besides, it's no different than the stretcher relay we ran at last year's Scout competition." Orlin was busy trimming side branches off of two long poles while the twins skinned some vines to use as rope.

"You guys *do* realize we each have rope, right?" Pete held up a coil of brightly-colored rope. The thin synthetic line was issued to each EESE student along with their camping gear.

"Actually, we should save that in case we have to lift or lower the travois," Orlin said as he started to lash sticks together to form the litter.

"Don't worry—"

"—we know—"

"—what we're doing—"

"—mostly."

It actually seemed as if they did know what they were doing. Their patrol, the Crockables, usually won troop competitions and had represented their troop many times in the regional games. When they weren't bickering, the boys worked well together. Pete decided he should gather some wide, flat leaves, and once the litter took shape, he and the twins wove a mat to cushion the injured human.

The travois worked the way it was supposed to, and the human twins, being the tallest of them, took turns pulling or lifting the litter as they headed for the ridge where they'd spend the night. When the trail became particularly steep, one of the twins would place the poles of the litter on his shoulders, and lift the downhill side while Orlin or Pete, being shorter, would take the uphill side. In this manner, they kept the still-unconscious stranger relatively level and free of bumps and jolts.

As evening approached, they found a campsite and set up much as they had the previous night. Jerry and Jinx donated some mosquito netting, and they rigged a tarp and netting around the litter for the night.

The next morning, the man stirred for a bit, and spoke in an odd language that their translators didn't recognize. His eyes didn't focus, and didn't really seem aware of his surroundings, so they weren't entirely sure that he wasn't simply delirious. The twins did manage to get him to drink some purified water and Pete contributed some of his protein paste.

"Do you think—"

"—we should break out The Brick?"

It was a concentrated emergency ration issued with the rest of their gear. The Marine who'd briefed them mentioned that it was the "only food supply they'd ever need to carry," mostly because "an intelligent being will eat *anything* before resorting to The Brick!" It was heavy and textured like an extremely dense bread or cake, and filled with small bits of fruit and nuts. It was extremely shelf-stable, and there were rumors of Bricks that had been handed down in certain families for generations.

"Ugh. No. Anything but the Brick. Besides, I don't have a chisel to break it into small enough pieces."

"We just thought—"

"—since we're using—"

"—your protein paste—"

"—that you might need something else!"

Pete shuddered. "No. No thanks, I can manage for another day."

"I wonder—"

"—does Brick go with curry?"

Pete shuddered again, and looked over at Orlin, who was doing his own version of rolling his eyes at the twins. He went to his pack and pulled out the EMT gloves again. He put a paw on the injured man, but noticed that he didn't see the normal head's-up display in his lower, right eye. He touched his cheek and the customary trace of nanites wasn't there. There were red lights flashing on the cuffs of both gloves, and he bent his left, lower eye—the one he usually used for fine detail—to read the tiny display.

Nanite supply exhausted, seek immediate medical attention.

That wasn't good. They still had today's descent to the equatorial plain, and then one more night before pickup. If he got any worse, they'd need to use the emergency beacon no matter what that did to their scores.

The sun was already down as they approached the location for the night's camp. They'd lost time when the stretcher lashings failed and they had to rebuild it. The downhill hike had been difficult. It was too rocky to drag the litter, so Orlin and Pete took turns carrying the uphill end, while the twins traded off with the downhill end. In the afternoon they'd come to the bank of a wide river. Pete's record of their course said that their goal was downstream, but across the river. There had been nothing in the briefing about crossing something that deep or swift, so they decided to follow the riverbank downstream for a while and hope that the river turned away from their direction of travel. After all, there was no sense in crossing the river only to discover they would have to cross back.

Sure enough, the river turned, and Pete recorded their position in his log. The destination should now be straight ahead, so even though it was getting late, they had a relatively clear path along the riverbank. They decide to press on to get absolutely as close as possible for the morning pick-up.

Much to their surprise, just as the last light was fading from the sky, they noticed artificial lights ahead and emerged from the densely forest of the past few days to an open plain, with the buildings of a large city on the far horizon. That must be Forest City, where they'd arrived four days ago. The lights they'd seen were from several military vehicles that appeared to be setting up a camp of their own.

Was this the extraction point? Had they accidently found the exact *spot they needed?*

A Prithmar Marine looked up and noticed the quartet walking out of the woods carrying the litter. "Well, well. You're early, but it looks like you've had a casualty."

Pete came to attention and saluted. "Cadet Corporal Pettekil Emil. We found an injured human and packed him out with us."

The soldier laughed. "At ease, Cadet. I'm a private, you don't need to salute. Private First Class Makk." When Pete relaxed, she approached and looked at the litter. "Hmm, well, you're here, so I guess that's good for him. Let me get a couple of stretcher bearers to get this one over to the medic trailer, I think they're just about set up. You might as well head over to the blue trailer. It's the check-in point. Not sure if being early is going to count against you, but no-one can fault your navigation. If you'd gotten here an hour earlier, you would have beaten us to the spot."

Ah. That explained it. Pete thought to himself. *They move in after dark when we're all supposed to be in camp. That way they don't give away the target coordinates.*

After a moment's thought, Pete figured he needed to stay in character as squad leader. "Cadets Orlin, Jerry and Jinx. Take the stretcher to the medic trailer. I will check us in."

The boys brought themselves to attention and saluted, much to the amusement of the Marine private. She nevertheless directed the boys toward the medic, and turned and saluted Pete with a smile. "I believe Top would say 'carry on' at this point, Cadet."

If the First Sergeant was surprised to see cadets in his camp one night early, he didn't show it. He took Pete's report, then examined the navigation logbook. He reached for his slate and tapped a few comments, then grunted. Looking up at Pete, he said, "Son, I've been running the EESE school of cadets for five years, and SERE school for Marines for the past decade. I have *never* had a squad turn up on my doorstep early. I *did* have to move the extraction point one course because a squad was camped about 50 meters away. They didn't have a watch set, though, and they woke up with our trucks and trailers surrounding them. It cost them a few points."

Pete felt his face begin to flush—despite his leathery skin—as he thought of the past two nights when all four of them had slept through the night. He continued to stand at attention, trying not to look directly at the first sergeant.

A faint hint of a smile appeared on the NCO's face. "I thought so," he said, "but that's a Marine thing, we don't worry about that too much with you cadets. Now, let's talk about your casualty..."

The next hours turned into an extensive debrief about when and where they'd found the injured human, and the decision to carry him out. Orlin, Jerry and Jinx were summoned to give their version, then the Marine doctor came in and questioned Pete about his first aid and field diagnosis. Pete didn't reveal that he had used the gloves from his EMT suit, but he was able to justify his decisions with the advanced first aid and field medicine he'd been studying on his own with the professors his cousin had introduced him to on Joth.

It was approaching midnight when the first sergeant and the captain-doctor seemed satisfied with the debrief. "Ok, Cadets. Private Makk will show you to the bunkhouse. You're here and you've had an unusual experience, so you might as well skip the tents for the night. I think there might be some chow in the mess tent as well. Dismissed." With that, the four headed for some welcome food. The mess tent had a plate of sandwiches suitable for humans and Caldivar, and a selection of pungent fruit for the Prithmar. They ate sparingly despite the long day, and stumbled off to their bunks.

The next morning the four squad mates ate a leisurely breakfast in the mess tent while listening to the sounds of increased activity in the camp. A few of the early EESE students staggered into the mess tent looking as if they hadn't eaten in three days. There was an increase in the general background noise as the ground-effect trucks moved out to pick up the squads that were more than a few kilometers away. They could also hear a flyer from time to time, and Pete didn't want to think about the number of points those squads would lose being so far off-course they needed to be picked up by air.

There was a roar of distant rockets. They went to one of the openings and looked out to see a drop-ship taking off.

Then again, there was off-course, and there was *Off. Course.*

Private Makk came in and headed for the coffee dispenser. She filled her canteen, then added lots of creamer and sugar. She smiled as she turned back and saw Pete and his squad.

"Was that—"

"—a dropship?"

Her smile slipped a bit into confusion at the twins' characteristic of finishing each other's sentences. Orlin and Pete were used to it, but it tended to take others by surprise. "Uh, yeah. Squad didn't make it past the valley. Three casualties out of a squad of five. Rescue's headed in to pick them up and transport straight back to Forest City." She took several long swigs from her canteen and topped it off from the coffee dispenser. "Oh, and Top told me that if I saw you four, to tell—let's see, how did he put it? Oh yeah. 'Send the med student to doc, he's gonna be short-handed. The other three might as well come over and help with check-in.' He also recommended that if you've got clean uniforms, put them on. All of the top scoring teams are already in, there's a few regular Marine squads out there that are still struggling. He gave me these for you to put on your uniforms to put the Marines in their place." She grinned, showing a mouthful of sharp teeth and held out a scaly paw holding four gold pins.

Those were EESE Honor Squad pins!

"I, I don't know what to say..." Pete trailed off, uncertain how to respond to the award.

"We do—"

"—we take it!" said Jinx and Jerry, immediately reaching for the pins.

Orlin reached for his pin, and Makk moved her paw just slightly, to make him fumble, then smiled and winked at him. Orlin's scales turned a faint yellow as he retrieved the pin, a Prithmar equivalent of a blush. Jinx—or Jerry—elbowed him in the ribs.

"...w-well, thank you," Pete finally said. "But I'm hardly a med student. We're all just finishing Upper."

"I heard Top and the Doc talking last night after you guys racked out. They were mighty impressed. Besides, Doc had to send two of his medics in the drop shuttle. You wouldn't believe how many cases of stomach upset and scale rot we see in the squads that come staggering in."

At that, all four of the squad flushed, and Makk just laughed. "A-HA! Yes, I see you know what I mean. Good thing you dealt with it before you got here. That's another point in your favor, you know."

Pete would have loved to accept the compliment, but he worried that using the EMT gloves would be considered cheating. It nagged at him that he might have actually endangered their standing in the guise of helping. He spoke quietly, trying not to betray the turmoil inside. "Uh, okay. We do have clean uniforms in our stored gear."

"Good, head over to the orange cargo units. They have your cubes, then report." She winked at Orlin again, and laughed once again at his discomfort. "Get going, heroes."

Pete felt even more conflicted. They weren't heroes. Even two years ago when he'd discovered The Suit and restored it, he was just a Scout trying to earn his

Maker Merit Badge. Today he felt like a kid pretending to be grown-up, while still making all of the mistakes of childhood.

After changing and putting the honor pins on their uniforms, Orlin, Jerry and Jinx headed off to the blue trailer to help with the check-in. There was already a line, and several Marines were setting up tables outside the mobile command center to handle the arriving squads.

Pete went over to the medical facility. The previous night it had been just a trailer pulled by a ground-effect truck. Today it was a complex of pop-up buildings and tents, and there were cadets and Marines standing, sitting, and lying on stretchers waiting for treatment. He was immediately put to work, although it was just minor stuff such as dispensing anti-fungal ointment and applying it to scale rot in places that the sufferer couldn't reach.

He wanted to ask the doctor about the man they'd brought in with them, but he didn't actually see the doc for a couple of hours. He heard the rockets as the dropship returned, and the two medics that had been dispatched returned and went to find the doc. The casualties had been delivered to the Forest City hospital, but Pete could see that one of the medics had blood on his uniform. A few minutes later, the medic and doctor—Captain Grisham—returned and came over to Pete.

"Son, we need you and your squad to come with us right away. Where is the rest of your squad?"

"O-over at the check-in. We were t-told to help out." *Was this it? Had they been found out and were about to be punished? Did something happen to the person they'd rescued?* "W-What's wrong, s-sir?"

"One of the other squads was attacked near where you found your casualty. We need to check over your log and pinpoint the exact location. We also need to find out if you saw anything else."

"Oh." It wasn't his worst fear, but it was still serious. He abruptly remembered his training. "Sir, yes, sir. Cadet Pete Emil at your command, sir." As he saluted, he saw a faint change in the doctor's expression, as if trying to remember something.

The doctor, medic and Pete headed over to the HG trailer, retrieving Orlin, Jerry and Jinx when they arrived. They could see the stern look on Pete's face, and kept their normal exuberance toned down. When they entered the office at the back of the trailer, Pete was surprised to see Top and a Caldivar wearing Colonel's insignia. Even with the efforts to end the xenophobic history of the Tretrayon military prior to the Salvage Fleet battles with the Squilla, non-humans were still rare in the upper levels of command.

The boys came to attention and saluted. The doctor and NCOs stood stiffly, but did not salute. Pete was worried that they had done something wrong, but the Colonel simply returned the salute and instructed them all to sit.

"Gentlemen," the senior officer began, "I am Colonel Alanatto. Doctor, I received your report, but I've just learned there is even more to the story." He turned and addressed Pete and the squad. "Boys, I have just learned that the human you found is wanted for kidnapping."

Pete, Orlin and the twins were shocked. Murmurs of "oh, no" and other words of dismay were exchanged.

Captain Grisham just nodded. "So, the shooting is probably related?"

The Colonel confirmed the doctor's statement and continued. "It happened within half a kilometer from your estimate of where you found the injured man. Your logbook, the tracker in your emergency beacon, and satellite surveillance gives us a kilometer radius as the likely site where he was hiding. The squad we airlifted out were Marines, and one of them said he'd rigged a sling and scored several hits while they were under fire."

"He had several contusions in addition to the scalp laceration. It's possible he was disoriented and wandered a bit before falling and hitting his head," the doctor supplied.

"The marine with the sling confirms that he heard an impact and a cry, then some thrashing about as the firing stopped. He would have given chase, but he had three wounded and only one other squad mate. They stayed in hiding for a day while they treated the wounds they best they could. When it proved impossible to make it to the extraction point today, they punched the rescue beacon."

For the next half hour, the boys were questioned about what they had seen in the area. Pete couldn't recall seeing any kind of shelter, but they *had* been approaching a stream, so perhaps the kidnapper had left his hideout in search of water.

The consensus was that they would simply have to mount a search and rescue mission. The man was accused of kidnapping the teen-aged daughter of local Caldivar councilman. He hadn't been identified as associated with known xenophobic organizations, but he had a record of petty crime that had advanced through extortion to armed robbery and now, kidnapping. There was a young lady, hidden out in the forest, and her food, water and health status were unknown.

The Colonel called for a fresh platoon of Marines—ones that had not been on the EESE course, as well as the Marines and cadets that had arrived earliest and had a chance to eat and rest. "That means you four will need to go back into the field. You found him, which means you hiked right past where he was likely hiding. We've got one of the Marines from the other squad. I don't dare put you in the front line of the search, it's too dangerous, but I want your eyes in the area." He looked directly at Pete and smiled. "All three of them."

The next item to plan was medic support. The later a squad arrived, the greater the number of injuries in the EESE students. In many cases, the reason for the delay *was* the health of the squad members. Captain Grisham would need most of his medics, and could only spare the one that had accompanied him to the meeting. "Besides, Cadet Pete has proven himself equal in skill to a basic medic. He seems to be a natural."

"Um, sirs." Pete hated to interrupt, knowing that what he was about to say could jeopardize their good standing with Top and the Colonel. "Do you have access to an EMT suit?"

"What? Why? We don't have anyone trained in them." The Colonel looked puzzled, but Captain Grisham got that same look that Pete had seen earlier.

"You do know that they have to be custom-fit and adapted to the wearer, right?" Top added.

"Yes, sir." Pete didn't even realize he'd called an NCO "sir" but no one else seemed to be paying attention. "But if you can get one, I can operate it."

Captain Grisham snapped his fingers as a look of understanding replaced the confusion on his face. "Pete Emil. Of clan -ekil, right? Pettekil Emil?"

"Yes, sir," Pete replied sheepishly.

The doctor turned and addressed his medic. "Specialist, there is an EMT Mark XI suit at Medical Command. Get on the horn and have them send it in a drop-pod. It's worth the expense." He turned back to Top and the Colonel as the medic saluted and left the office. "Gentlemen, this young Cadet is Pete Emil. The 'Emil' in 'Emil Medical Tool.' He *invented* the EMT suit!"

"Actually, sir, I just recovered it."

"Recovered, discovered, identified, reassembled, reconditioned, decoded and then demonstrated field capability on first use." He laid a hand on Pete's shoulder. "Once my suit gets here, Pete will be as good as any doctor or field surgeon." He paused a moment, then continued, "the only problem is that I don't have gloves for a Caldivar."

"I, uh, might have my own."

"*I knew it!* Specialist Murphy owes me a beer. A squad that comes in with no sign of bad water or fungus? You know they cheated the odds somehow."

"I'm sorry, sir, does that mean we're disqualified?" There was an ache in Pete's stomach right now.

"The Captain said *'cheating the odds'* Cadet, not 'cheating.' This is supposed to be a realistic exercise, and Marines are all about every edge we can get. Just ask President Tomeral." The Colonel laughed, but then turned serious. "Still, I have to ask you. Cadet, are you up to this?" He stared at Pete intently with his upper eye.

Pete stood as straight and tall as he possibly could, executed as precise a salute as he knew how, and replied, "Yes, sir."

The Colonel nodded and returned the salute. "Then make it so."

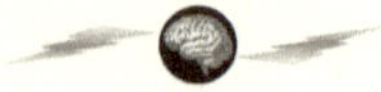

The dropship delivered the augmented platoon of thirty marines, plus Top, the Marine EESE student, and Pete's squad to the side of the river a bare fifty meters form the point they'd found the injured man. Each of the five EESE students was pared with an NCO, and Pete had drawn the First Sergeant—or Top had drawn Pete, he wasn't sure which was which.

"Okay, Cadet, show me where you found him." Pete noted that Top and the regular Marines were armed and armored. The Cadets had been warned to stay down and undercover if any shooting started. Pete student pointed out the slight depression where they'd found the man, the blood-stained rock was still there. Top called over the Marine EESE student who confirmed that the rock was *not* one that he'd launched from his make-shift sling. It was too big to be slung, but a bit small for the man to have simply fallen on.

However, it was not too big to have been wielded by hand.

"Okay, Cadet. You'd better suit up." Pete was wearing the carapace, legs and sleeves of a new manufacture EMT suit. It was certainly cleaner than the one he'd refurbished two years before. This one came with a display monocle built into a pair of goggles, since most users were discomfited by nanites crawling up their cheek and forming interface nodes in the ear and eye. The monocle was designed for a human, though, so rather than don the headset to activate the suit, Pete merely donned his gloves, and allowed them to tap into the seemingly limitless nanite supply of the never-before-used suit.

The head's-up display in front of his lower, right eye made an interesting overlay with the close-up view from his lower, left eye, and the distance view of his upper eye. Not only did the display identify two types of blood on the rock, it indicated two trails of blood leading away from the site, one downhill toward the river and one uphill.

"First Sergeant, there's two blood trails leading away, which one should we follow?"

"We follow both, Cadet. That's why we have a platoon with us."

"Oh, yes, sir."

The NCO turned and looked at the cadet intensely, raising one eyebrow.

"Sorry, s—First Sergeant!"

"Cadet, you have certainly earned the right to call me 'Top'—just so long as you don't call me 'sir.'"

"Yes, Top. Understood." Pete thought a moment. "Top, I can track one trail with my head's-up display, but no-one can see the other trail. I can charge the human-interface monocle with nanites and then they can follow the other trail."

"Good thinking." He motioned the other senior NCO over. "Gunny, take a squad. Detail one man as tracker and have them wear the goggles. Your squad heads..." He looked at Pete, and the latter pointed down toward the river bank. "...toward the river. We'll go up this way."

The platoon separated, with squads heading in the two directions *not* associated with a blood trail as well, and formed up in search lines to make sure there was no-one else in the area besides the one who had been bleeding. Orlin was with the gunnery sergeant's squad, and Pete was amused to see Private Makk wearing the tracker as they moved out. Jerry and Jinx had been separated and would each be in one of the teams paralleling the river. Pete led the way as Top's squad moved uphill away from the river, back in the direction from which his team had come just two days ago.

For an hour, they moved carefully through the forest, both on and off of the trail that Pete's squad had traveled. The nine members of their squad spread out in a line perpendicular to their direction of travel. They were spaced about ten meters apart, except for Top, who stayed glued to Pete's side. Pete could still detect faint traces of blood, when Top's radio crackled. Gunny's team—and Orlin—had found a shack with signs that someone had been held there. That person—presumably the councilman's daughter—had apparently cut through her restraints with the sharp edge of a rock, probably the same one she'd later used to knock the kidnapper unconscious. The blood trail ended there, although the squad would continue to search that area just in case there was another kidnapper waiting to see if anyone returned.

That meant that the girl had to be in the direction Pete was tracking.

It was another hour before Pete lost the blood trail. He backtracked and picked it up again, then lost it once more as he headed back uphill. He turned around and carefully searched the edges of the trail.

"This way," he called, and headed off the trail.

They found her ten minutes later, a female Caldivar, maybe a year younger than Pete. Her clothes were torn, and her tough skin was scuffed and scratched. Her upper eye was bruised and swollen, and she was curled in a ball at the base of a tree. It appeared that she had attempted to climb the tree, as her claws were extended, and there were scratches in the tree bark. Alas, Caldivar were a burrowing species, and tree climbing was something that took considerable practice—Pete knew how only because he'd grown up with the human twins. Even if she'd succeeded in climbing the tree, she would not have been able to get her bearings this far into the forest.

As soon as Pete looked at the girl, his EMT display started showing yellow and red caution indicators. She was dehydrated and malnourished, it had apparently been three days since she had eaten. Her left ankle was sprained, and there was a broken bone at the wrist joint of her left paw. Either she'd injured both at the same time, or the wrist injury had occurred when she broke free of her restraints. She also had lacerations at the wrists, and they appeared to be infected.

With Top's help, Pete got the unconscious girl uncurled and got the carapace of the EMT suit onto her. Top grunted in surprise to see it shrink and conform to her. Even though she was close to Pete's age, she was quite a bit smaller. He'd seen it before with members of his extended family that lived in the city. Country boys grew to almost the height of a human, but city Caldivar tended to be shorter.

Pete's suit interface also instructed him to remove his left leg sleeve and place it on the girl, whereupon it inflated into a cast and immobilized the ankle. He examined her wrists, and the gloved exuded antiseptic-anesthetic nanites into the wounds.

Once Pete indicated that treatment was complete for now, Top gathered the girl up in his arms and carried her back to the trail, then downhill to where they'd started. The other three teams reported that there was no-one else in the area, and Top summoned everyone back to the muster point. The last arrived just as the drop-ship arrived.

They flew directly to the hospital in town, delivered the girl to her family and the doctors on-site, then headed back to the EESE camp. Pete and his squad mates were due to catch a shuttle back to Joth at midnight, and they still needed to pack and catch a meal before heading to the spaceport. Top came to see them off, and apologized that he was unable to escorted them himself, but he assigned Private Makk to fly them over to Forest City. Pete noted that Orlin managed to snag the front seat, so that he could talk with the female Prithmar. Pete rode in the back with a couple of other EESE students and the twins, Jerry and Jinx, who were unusually subdued, although they got into an argument with the other students about the latest video by a band called Cypress Spring. He sat back and closed all three eyes, thinking of a young female Caldivar who would have been quite pretty if she hadn't been so sick and injured.

Word got back to both their Scout troop and their classmates in the Upper school that they had scored Honor Squad in the Extreme Environment Survival Exercise. There was a commendation from Colonel Alanatto and a personal letter of recommendation for Pete signed by Captain—Doctor—Grisham and Top. Pete was surprised to see that Top signed the letter 'Edward Stacey.' It turned out that Top was a cousin of Evelyn Stacey—head of Salvage System's Navy and President Tomeral's fiancée. The boys had gained a lot of attention, but thankfully, it passed, and they were able to get back to work and finish their final year of Upper on Joth before heading off to the Academy.

One week before graduation, the class was supposed to report for Award Assembly. The various academic and sport awards would be announced, along with the class rankings for valedictorian and honors. They had been instructed to wear their cadet uniforms, but that was because their entire cadet class had earned honors from the drill exhibition earlier in the spring. Thus, it was a surprise to Pete when he saw First Sergeant Stacey and Colonel Alanatto file in behind the school officials and representatives of the various awarding agencies.

Something was up.

The sight of Doctor Grisham, and an unknown Caldivar clinched it. The Marines were all in dress uniform, and the Caldivar was in a formal suit that looked almost military.

Near the end of the assembly, but before the valedictorian announcement, Colonel Alanatto got up and called for Pete, Orlin, Jerry and Jinx. Understanding that military decorum was in order, they marched in formation to the stage and lined up facing Top.

"Last summer, these four cadets distinguished themselves, not only by earning Honor Squad at the summer Extreme Environment Survival Exercise on Tretra, but also demonstrated courage and commitment by rescuing and extracting an injured civilian while earning that honor." Colonel Alanatto addressed the assembly, while Top marched to the table at center stage and retrieved four flat, black boxes. "In addition, these young men participated in the search and rescue effort for Susanatto Onid, a young girl lost in the same area used by the EESE school."

Lost. That was interesting. No mention that it was a kidnapper or that the man they 'rescued' was the kidnapper, Pete thought to himself. *Wait, Susanatto? Clan -atto, just like the Colonel?*

The Colonel had continued speaking, and Pete's attention was caught by his next words, "...upholding the best tradition of both Cadets and Marines. For these actions, Cadets Orlin, Jerry Garcia, Jinx Garcia and Pettekil are awarded the Cadet Star." The assembly applauded and the Colonel waited until it died down before continuing. "And for the record, not only is this the first time the Star has been awarded *on* Joth, Cadets Orlin and Pete are the first Prithmar and Caldivar to earn this honor."

The assembly came to its feet as Top pinned the miniature stars to their uniforms and Colonel Alanatto came over to salute and shake their hands. As the audience was seated, Top dismissed the other three, but motioned for Pete to remain.

Captain Grisham stepped to the microphone. "Cadet Pettekil Emil. Your home world of Joth surely knows the role you have played in finding the lost technology of the EMT suit and bringing its capability back to our troops and hospitals. Ladies and Gentlemen, we have an additional award to present today. Councilor Cubinatto Onid."

The civilian Caldivar stepped up. "Cadet Pete, when my brother, Colonel Alanatto informed me that my daughter was rescued by a Cadet from Joth, I was interested. When Doctor Grisham told me that Susa's rescuer was the Caldivar who had discovered the EMT suit, I was intrigued. When I further learned of your aptitude for medicine, I asked my family what we could do for you in return. Alan tells me you are headed to the Academy, but have not yet chosen a track. Doc says if you don't choose flight surgeon, it would be a waste, so clan -atto has established a scholarship to Forest City College of Medicine, to commence in your second year at Academy." Once again, the audience stood and applauded.

The councilman stepped back and motioned to a young female standing just off the stage. She stepped up and handed over a large rigid folder. She then turned toward Pete and winked her lower left eye.

It was her!

Her father continued, "...This certificate with my family's thanks." He bowed to the audience, then father and daughter stepped over beside Colonel Alanatto and Top, and all four bowed to Pete.

Pete returned the bow, and as he straightened, he noticed that Susa was staring at him again. Once she knew he was looking, she winked at him again. He caught a very stern look from her uncle, the colonel, but that, too, dissolved into a smile and a wink.

Pete's head was spinning, he barely noticed that the Principal didn't allow him to sit down before they announced the valedictorian. He was a good student; he just hadn't realized he had done that well.

I wonder if it's the nanites? Is that cheating? No, it's just cheating the odds!
***

RESCUE OPS

Authors note: Pete, Orlin, Jerry, and Jinx are no longer boys. Pete has graduated from medical school, and the others have entered military service, like many of the Scouts I knew. Pete's EMT suit gives him an advantage as a medic and doctor – so where does a man with a talent for rescue end up? In Rescue Operations, obviously!.

Join Medical Command. Travel the Universe. Meet new people... and HELP them!

Pettekil Emil stared at the sign for several minutes before continuing into the multistory building labeled Salvage-Coalition Medical Command. Pete was a Caldivar from Joth, the "minor" planet of the Tretra System. For hundreds of years, the human inhabitants of Tretra had dominated the system's military and professions. That all changed when the Squilla invaded, and the Tretra military were rescued by a group of misfits from the desert planet of Joth. It was an eye-opening experience, and Tretra soon learned that the humans, lizard-like Prithmar and anteater-like Caldivar had much to offer—particularly since Harmon Tomeral, leader of those misfits, forced the Tretra leadership to face—and demolish—their own prejudices.

Following the example of independence shown by Tomeral, Pete and his best friends, Orlin—a Prithmar—as well as Jerry and Jinx—human twins—had been looking for spare parts they could assemble into working machines of their own design for their Maker Merit Badge when he discovered a piece of Lost Technology—an Emergency Medical Tool mecha—also known as the EMT Mark XI. Two years later, Pete, Orlin, Jerry and Jinx were undergoing an extreme environment survival experience as Cadets training for the Tretray-on—and eventually Salvage—military academy. They encountered an unconscious human, treated his injuries, and carried the injured man for several days to their extraction point. Upon learning that the man was wanted for kidnapping, and that his victim was likely still up on the mountainside where he'd been found, they joined in the search party to rescue the daughter of a local Caldivar politician.

He was hailed as a genius for the first event, and a hero for the second, but in the Academy, he was simply "not half bad." The scholarship to Forest City Medical School on Tretra, a reward courtesy of the family of Susa, the girl he'd rescued, resulted in his recent graduation as a Doctor of Trauma Medicine, and a captain in the Salvage Marines Medical Command.

Through this door would be the career that would shape the *rest* of his life.

If only he could convince himself that he was ready.

His orders said to report to Colonel Suminto, and he was directed to a door at the far end of the room. He made his way through the busy office, knocked on the door, and heard a voice inviting him to enter.

"Captain Doctor Pettekil Emil, reporting for duty." Pete stood at his best parade-ground attention and snapped a sharp salute, the digits of his right paw just barely brushing the lid of his long-distance eye, centered above the two eyes he typically used for near-field and fine-focus purposes.

Colonel Suminto was a Rincah, a member of another humanoid race with ram-like features and curved horns on his head. Salvage System, and the Coalition they'd formed, was unique in the outer worlds by virtue of the sheer diversity of the society—and in particular, it's armed forces. It made learning to be a flight surgeon all that more challenging, but Pete had a slight advantage in that his EMT suit had a near artificial intelligence programmed to recognize and diagnose over one-thousand races. He didn't let that stop him from learning as much as he could without "cheating" through the use of his own compact EMT-link.

Suminto stood as Pete came to attention. He walked around the desk, returned Pete's salute, and offered his hand to shake. Pete was surprised to see that he towered over the commanding office. "Captain Emil. Welcome to Rescue Ops. I've heard good things about you. Top of your class, quick thinker, hard worker. I trust the Academy disabused you of those 'hero' notions the popular media like to throw around."

"Yes sir, the Academy and medical school showed me just how much I didn't know."

"Good." The colonel told Pete to be at ease, and gestured to a chair beside the desk. Suminto took a chair where he could sit in a comfortable conversational manner. "You'll find out that Rescue Ops views you in a slightly more favorable light. We want you here precisely because of the qualities you've shown us. Part of your time will be spent developing the Mark XII EMT and part of it will be continuing your education in order to become fully board- and flight-certified.

"I'm telling you this, because you're getting dropped right in the thick of it. I know you have your own personal Mark XI EMT, reconditioned from the original parts, so you'll need some updates. In two days you're going out on a mission."

"A mission? Already? I thought I was supposed to spend two years in residency?"

"You do, and you will. The two-year practicum cannot be waived, but with your experience, we can rotate you in and out of assignments that complement the battlefield and emergency medicine training you're supposed to be getting. We need you, more importantly, we need your suit and your experience with it."

"Sir, uh... thank you, sir."

"I'm not so sure you should thank me, yet. We provide assistance to those who've gotten a raw deal from the Galaxy... and it's in those circumstances that Rescue Ops plays a major role."

"Disaster relief?"

"Got it in one. The Akea system is having a comet problem. A rather large, rocky object entered their system, headed toward the sun, then broke into smaller pieces. They've already had several large strikes as their planet passed through the tail of the comet on its way sunward, and they're likely to get hit by more fragments. Akea will be right in the comet's path as it heads back out."

Pete thought for a moment, considering parabolic and elliptic trajectories, interplanetary speeds, and other variables. It was the sort of thing Jerx—Jerry and Jinx, that is—were very good at. Pete was no slouch at math, but the exercise made his head hurt. "That's... highly improbable, sir. A comet on a parabolic trajectory should round the sun much faster than a planet on round or even elliptical orbit."

"Ah, good. Your record said you were sharp. We don't know if it's natural from the outgassing, or something else. Either way, we have two months to rescue, relocate or assist the Akeans. Floods, earthquakes, volcanic eruptions, acid rain... lots of injured people, and we don't know enough about the race—they're not in any of our databases. We're hoping they're in yours."

"Uh... thank you? Sir?"

Suminto laughed. "Oh, you're going to love it here, son. Never a dull moment!"

After Pete left Colonel's office, he proceeded down to the laboratory on the twelfth level. As he walked into the lab, he noticed one of the technicians was a Eitom –an eight-foot-tall humanoid with heavy build and three arms. The biology of the Eitom showed that they'd once had four arms, but the upper and lower arms on the left side had fused together. On the right side, a normal sized upper arm concealed a delicate lower arm that generally folded in underneath the upper.

Pete had met an Eitom from one of the early years in his medical training. Eddie was one year ahead of him in medical school. Much to his surprise, the Eitom looked up as he entered the laboratory and addressed him by name. "Hey, Pete, glad to see you finally made it!"

"Wow, Eddie, I'm surprised to see you here!"

"Don't be, we always talked about your EMT, and this is the best place to work on one. I get to do medicine and fiddle with gadgets at the same time. Did you even *read* your assignment orders?"

Pete's three eyes opened wide, and he pulled out the thin plastic sheet that constituted his official orders. He snapped to attention and spoke a tight, "Yes, sir, Major Niveen, sir!"

"At ease, Pete. We are pretty informal, and this is just the lab. You can still call me Eddie unless there's a superior officer present, like the Colonel."

"Uh. Thanks, Eddie." Pete put his carryall on a benchtop and pulled out silvery cloth and a hardshell chest plate. "The Colonel said you need my EMT for something—but not a whole lot else about what to expect other than this urgent rescue operation."

"Okay, well, Rescue Ops is just what it sounds like. We provide search and rescue support to Tetra, Salvage System and Coalition worlds. It's just like an emergency medicine residency. " Eddie pulled over a computer link cable and plugged it into the primary interface console built into the hardshell. He then unlatched small cylinders attached to the backplate and connected them to a machine against one wall of the laboratory. "*This* is where we finally put it all to use. We go out in the community and into the galaxy, working rescues, disasters, and recovery. *This* is when it gets fun."

"Wow. I'm not sure what I was expecting. Classrooms, simulators, maybe bandaging training injuries or other minor stuff. This is ... fast, I guess is what I want to say."

"Well, the planet we're headed to, Akea—actually, the major race calls themselves Carico –caused a stir because they're not in any of our databases. That means we're going in on a rescue without detailed medical knowledge. Med Command is hoping that we can get some translations once your suit recognizes the Carico and that might just help us pull out more translations from your database."

"Aye-aye, Major Eddie!" Pete threw a quick salute and smiled.

"Not under cover, soldier," Eddie replied, but grinned as he said it. "Yeah, you'll fit in just fine."

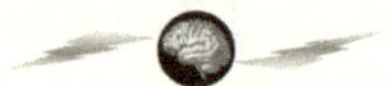

Pete was billeted in the visiting officer's quarters. That seemed strange, he certainly didn't feel like an officer. After dinner, he returned to quarters, pulled out his slate and started re-reading his orders and dealing with a large number of comm messages he'd received since officially arriving. Once all of that was done, he sent a quick text to his mother, letting her know he'd arrived and all was well. She'd appreciate that. Next was a somewhat longer text to Susa. They'd seen a lot of each other when he had breaks in med school. He missed her already, and knew that she was waiting for word whether he'd be returning soon, or she should come join him.

After composing and sending a lengthy message with lots of reassurances, but carefully worded to keep her from racing to join him, Pete laid down on the strange bunk and tried to sleep... not that it would do any good, he could seldom fall asleep immediately with such an important day ahead of...

... He was awake before his alarm. The yellow-orange light of Salvage System's primary had awoken him the moment the sun cleared the distant hills. Every morning on Tretra at the Academy and med school, he'd awoken with the dawn. Growing up on Joth, residents were up several hours before dawn to take advantage of the relative coolness—sleeping until dawn always seemed like a luxury...

This upcoming mission gave Pete a strange feeling in his stomach. It took a while to recognize it—but eventually he realized that it was the same feeling he'd had twice before—the first time when he'd worn the newly refurbished Mark XI EMT to rescue his injured friends on Joth, and the other time when he'd been tasked with locating Susa when she'd been kidnapped. Anticipation, excitement... whatever. It was time to knuckle down and do the job he'd been training for the past seven years.

Pete met the rest of the team the next day. Rescue Ops was a large organization with hundreds of members working all across the galaxy. The Salvage office was largely research and headquarters support, but the evacuation of Akea would require every possible technician, medic, doctor and rescuer. While waiting for Pete and his EMT Mark XI, Colonel Suminto had sent everyone else off to Akea. In addition to Pete, Eddie and the colonel, there was Ralph, a cyber-canid from Earth; Walicta, a platypus-like Otreme; and Serena, a human female who was their Marine security specialist.

Walicta—Eddie called her 'Wally'—just nodded and waved a clawed forepaw in Pete's direction. Serena stuck out her hand to shake Pete's paw with a quick, forceful motion. Ralph, however, walked up to Pete on all fours, stood on his back legs and embraced him in a hug. " Glad you could join us, Pete," the cybernetically-enhanced canine spoke through a translator positioned over his throat.

"Ralph is our 'digital nose.' He can sense the chemicals given off by living creatures with a sensitivity much greater than any race could manage without assistance. He's also our practical joker and comic relief. Wally is the penetration expert. She can explore small spaces and carry relief supplies to anyone trapped in collapsed buildings, cave-ins and wreckage. Serena will run security, although we'll be augmented with at least one mecha." Eddie handled the introductions since the Colonel had been called back into a conference call. "We'll also have a couple of dropships we can call on. We'll be needing one for our team, and another will deliver the Marines that will work with Serena."

Pete wondered if those marines might include his friends Orlin, Jerry and Jinx. Orlin had gone into mechanized infantry. The nearly inseparable twins, Jerry and Jinx, had entered flight school. It would be nice to see them, but he knew the odds did not favor it.

Colonel Suminto returned from his office and addressed the group. "Our departure has been moved up. We leave this afternoon. I just got off the comm with Admiral Lurvel who is in command in the Akea system. That comet has a lot of fragments. There have been some major meteor strikes in the past day, and they need all hands, immediately. Our gear and the three EMTs are on the way to the transport as we speak; you have one hour to collect personal gear, and another thirty minutes to get to Yatarward Field. We lift in one-hundred-twenty minutes. Now go."

Fortunately, Pete hadn't really unpacked, so he was able to grab a clean uniform, some utilizes, and one of the new lightweight, reinforced jumpsuits to wear under the EMT. He still had time to spare, so he decided to hit the 'fresher himself, and get to the field early.

There was a drop ship on the field displaying a logo of an angel holding a globe. The shuttle itself had its numerical designation and name—347-38D Cunningham—but was also emblazoned with the name of its parent ship—CRO Takur Gar. Standing at the cockpit door was a human with red-hair and a familiar freckled face. Although he'd grown taller and thinner, Jerry still had the irrepressible smile that Pete remembered from his younger days.

"Jerry!"

"Pete! Hey, Jinx is not going to believe this!"

"Wow. That's not right, you finishing your own sentences."

"I know—" Jerry paused for a moment then grinned and continued, "—strange, isn't it? My worse half went for fighters, I had the aptitude for dropships, the Navy finally managed to find a difference between us."

"But, do you still see each other?"

"Oh sure, we're both stationed on the Mayaguez. I'm just on loan to the Takur Gar for this mission. The only real difference between the bomb truck he drives and the bus I drive is that the weapons I deploy can think for themselves."

"Hah! And what does Jinx say to that?"

"Usually something about not having to worry about shaking up the cargo if he does a barrel roll."

"Yup, that sounds like Jinx."

"C'mon in and get your gear stowed. We've got some Caldivar seats up near the bulkhead."

Eddie was the next to show up, followed by Wally, Ralph, and then Serena. Colonel Suminto showed up at exactly ninety minutes after he'd sent the team to pack. He was wearing a commander's comm helmet, and seemed to still be in conference as the dropship spooled up its engines and lifted off.

The Takur Gar was typical for a naval support ship—lots of cargo and shuttle space, tiny crew quarters. In fact, the quarters had to be allocated according to species' size. Thus, Eddie and the Colonel would be one deck up on the Rincah-Yalteen deck, while Pete and the others were quartered on the Human deck. Pete shared a half-compartment with Ralph, while Serena and Wally shared the other half, behind a flexible divider that Wally insisted would be kept closed to "keep the boys out." The massive cargo decks were almost completely empty—reserved for whatever was needed to evacuate anyone and anything from Akea.

There was barely enough time to secure their carryalls in the restraint webbing and strap into their bunks before the acceleration alarm sounded and they began a three-gee burn to get to the stargate, and thus to Akea as fast as they possibly could.

"Alert! All personnel to duty stations. Alert!"

Pete jumped up out of his bunk and hit his head on the low bulkhead. He rolled over and slid down to the floor, eliciting a yelp from Ralph. "Oh man, I'm sorry. I didn't mean to land on your tail!"

"It's okay, Pete. I'll be sure to return the favor." Ralph grinned with a very doglike expression and cocked his head sideways. The action was accompanied by laughter from his collar-mounted translator. "Seriously, though. It was my fault. I was asleep and jumped up like a newbie."

Pete rubbed his head and didn't say anything. Ralph looked back at him, then cocked his head to the other side and 'yipped' in time with the laughter coming from the miniature speaker.

"We'd better suit up. Our duty stations are right here until the Colonel tells us otherwise—but if the alarms are going off, we need to be ready to deploy when he does call."

Pete was already in the silky skin suit he'd packed in the top of his carryall. All personnel onboard ship were required to wear some form of vacuum-resistant clothing. Most wore shipsuits, a type of skin suit with light insulation that could be sealed to a variety of footwear, helmets and gloves. Pete's was meant to be worn under his EMT and only worked with custom gloves and helmet that were extensions of the EMT itself. He'd made his own gloves for the cadet survival school, and customized a helmet for his three eyes and elongated snout. It also had an interface for the EMTs specialized nanites that formed visual and auditory display interfaces over his eyes and ears.

Pete suited up, then turned to assist Ralph. The cybernetically-uplifted canine found it almost impossible to sleep in any form of body covering, and needed to get into a garment with reinforced weave that served as both pressure suit and armor. Eddie had offered to shave him prior to deployment, but Ralph preferred to keep his thick gold-and-white-colored fur. That made getting into the skin suit more difficult, especially in a hurry, so he'd made his bunkmate promise to assist since Pete didn't need as much time to suit up. The worst part—for Pete—was that Ralph's tail wagged when he was excited, making it all the more difficult to get him completely encased in the suit.

Once Ralph was safely suited, with no fur caught in the seals, Pete finished donning his EMT. The main body plate was a clamshell that fit over his chest and back, plus arm and leg sleeves that connected to tubing and wiring sockets on the clamshell. The suit morphed itself to fit his body, then cover shoulders, hips and groin, leaving no portion of Pete unprotected. He felt nanites assembling a diagnostic monocle in his lower right eye, and a display formed in his vision that echoed the heads-up display in his helmet.

It only took two minutes for Pete and Ralph to be completely sealed and armored. Almost as soon as they finished, the partition retracted to reveal Wally was in a small cylinder with tank treads and articulated external arms, and Serena in a shipsuit with added marine scout armor.

Their Rescue Ops squad looked ready. His helmet comm activated, and he heard Colonel Suminto's voice. "Team, report to shuttle bay twelve. SKY-WATCH is reporting cometary fragments in the emergence zone. We are sending out all dropships immediately."

At that very moment, they felt and heard an impact shake the ship. More alarms started to go off, and the external atmosphere indicator in his helmet started to alternate green and yellow. The four looked at each other for a moment, then—as they had practiced in the drills, Pete reached down and picked up Wally, tucking her little tank under his left arm, while Serena picked up Ralph and hoisted him up to drape over her shoulders. With the smallest—and slowest—members of the team now riding, they set off for shuttle bay twelve as fast as they could.

In the shuttle bay Pete could see mecha-suited marines loaded onto two largest shuttles, while EMT suited medics and various scouting species loaded into smaller dropships. There was a sense of urgency, and many support personnel were added to the vessels at the last minute.

The Takur Gar shuddered under an impact, and Pete's ears popped. Emergency alarms started and sounded a depressurization warning. More impacts were felt and the loading crews forced people onto the shuttles under the strobing red light of emergency evacuation beacons. Eddie led the team to the Cunningham, where the pilot didn't even wait for all of the occupants to get strapped in before closing the hatch and moving to the bay exit.

Another impact shook the Takur Gar as Jerry's voice came over the compartment speakers and suit intercoms. "If you're seated, stay there, anyone standing, either sit on the floor or strap yourselves to the cargo rings on the walls. This is going to be rough."

Pete felt the shuttle rotate relative to the direction that had been "down" on the Gar, then the shuttle's belly-mounted thrusters throttled up and pushed everyone toward the floor of the compartment. He gave a silent command consisting of subvocalization and muscle twitches to his EMT, and a display opened in his view, courtesy of the nanites now concentrated in front of his lower right eye. He selected a visual feed from the external sensors on Gar and Cunningham.

The view of Gar was shocking, with obvious impacts glowing a bright yellow from heat. As he watched, another bloom appeared right over the shuttle bay and he could see shuttle jets firing erratically and fragments coming off of a ship that had been directly behind them exiting the bay. Pete wanted to scan around to find the source of the projectiles impacting the ship, but Jerry came over the comm to warn the passengers to expect evasive maneuvers. Pete commanded the display to turn off, sat back, and tightened his straps. The next ten minutes were harrowing, as their pilot put the dropship into spins, abrupt changes in direction, and alternating high acceleration and braking. As the violent movements began to slack off, the comm channel chimed with a high priority incoming transmission.

"All Rescue Ops personnel. Please switch to Command Channel Alpha-Seven for a message from Admiral Lurvel." The EMT comm system automatically switched, but Pete knew that some of the additional persons who'd been packed onto the dropship might not have been tuned into unit-specific comms.

"All personnel—if you are listening to this broadcast, you know that the Takur Gar is currently under emergency and has initiated evacuation protocols. Gar emerged from gate transit into a debris cloud that has been attribute to the rogue comet threatening the planet Akea. The cometary debris is small in size, radar transparent and low albedo. It was not detected until the Gar was right in the debris cloud. We have loaded as many of the support personnel onto the dropships and shuttles as possible, and all unattached personnel should report to Base Green for assignment. Rescue Ops operational squads will receive assignments via chain-of-command once you are groundside.

"Rest assured, the Takur Gar is not out of this. We have offloaded Coalition personnel for resource and safety reasons. By the time we are ready to complete the evacuation of Akea, we expect to have the Gar back in operation." There was text information about the assignment of the bases and attaching the various shuttles and dropships to the and different operational groups. Base Green would act as the main hospital and processing center for Carico that needed to be evacuated from unsafe or heavily damaged areas. There were bases for urban rescue, suburban and rural operations, and high-latitude polar regions. Base White served as a headquarters unit for the marine commanding general and Colonel Suminto's team.

As Pete was reading, he felt the aft engines throttle up for the transition to Akean orbit, and then landing. He figured this was as good a time as any to refresh his information on Rescue Ops procedures and any information they had on the Carico. It seemed like there would not be any time to spare once they landed. Thus, it seemed no time at all until atmospheric buffeting began, and then suddenly seemed to stop as the engines wound down.

He was seized by a moment of panic.

Had the engines failed? Were they dropping from a great height to end of crushed on the surface?

It was only when he noticed the other occupants unbuckling their restraints and beginning to move around the cabin, that he realized they had landed. Once more, he was caught up in the seeming chaos and haphazard process of getting all of the additional persons off of the dropship but soon found himself joined by Serena and Ralph—Wally's tank was still secured above his left shoulder—and then by Eddie and Colonel Suminto.

"Follow me. We need to get comms and databases set up in headquarters first. Billeting will come later—we're likely getting cots in a back room, because we're going to be *busy*!" True to his word, the Colonel had them working integrating communications with all of the rescue teams and setting up the computer systems and medical databases until well after local nightfall. Given that Base White was located at a northern latitude during local summer, that was late indeed. Pete estimated that it had been at least thirty hours since they'd awoken to alarms on the Gar. It was the first of many long days, and each night he laid down on his cot and fell asleep without delay.

Pete woke to movement near his cot. The entire headquarters staff—including the colonel—were bunked in a large room behind the main staff room. The females were on the other side of an opaque curtain, although shadows indicated that someone was also moving on that side.

Eddie touched him on the shoulder and whispered, "Time to get moving, Pete, you are headed down to base Green today to see if we can get some more information about the Carico out of your EMT."

He blinked several times, and the nanites in front of his eye reconfigured into a messaging display. Sure enough, he had new orders telling him to report to Base White's airfield at o500.

He checked his chrono. It had been local midnight when all but the night watch had headed to their cots. It was now 0430—what doctors and marines commonly called "oh-dark-thirty." He had thirty minutes to get ready. Fortunately, he'd started sleeping wearing a glove, leg or sleeve of his EMT, so that he had nanites available in an emergency. A silent command started them performing perform basic hygiene. It had been very useful in medical school to have flush fatigue toxins from his body after a long procedure or late night of studying.

He was surprised to learn that Serena was going to be accompanying him to Base Green. When he asked Eddie about it, he was told that she was assigned as security. He and his suit were considered high-value assets—well, technically, his suit had the high value, but as the most knowledgeable user, he came in a close second in value. Therefore, he merited an escort who would do her best to keep him out of trouble whenever he was out of HQ.

He was even more surprised to learn that he would be traveling to Green not in a shuttle or dropship, but in the back seat of a fighter. Two Marine Q-114 were waiting for Pete and Serena at the landing pad. Their engines were spooled up to a fast idle, and as soon as the airfield technicians strapped him into the back seat, the canopy closed and they rolled out to the runway. He was pushed back into his seat by g-forces as the pilot pointed the nose at the sky and accelerated straight up, followed by a loop and barrel roll. The comm crackled, "quit showing off, Red Five. Captain Emil is not going to be impressed."

"Hey, that was just evasive maneuvers, Red Leader," said the pilot. The voice sounded familiar.

"Jinx?" Pete asked.

"At your service, Pete. Red Flight delivery, you spy 'em, we fly 'em."

"Not that I'm not happy to see you—but, why you? Why fighters—wouldn't a shuttle make more sense?"

"Not really, not for two people, plus the orbitals are pretty busy right now. Atmospheric is better, faster, and appropriate for single or double cargo."

"So, I'm cargo now?"

"Hey, do I look like a trash hauler... no, don't answer that. Yeah, you're cargo. Valuable cargo. They need you at Green A-S-A-P."

"I TOLD Jerry that it was odd to hear him speaking in complete sentences. I think it might be even stranger from you."

Jinx laughed. "Yeah, basic broke us of a lot of things. Okay, hold on, we've got some bad weather ahead and we've been vectored through instead of over or around. It's going to get rough, but Red Leader and I are going to pour on some speed and bring up the combat shields. That should take the extreme edges off of the turbulence."

True to his word, the ride got extremely rough. Mach-plus flight through the center of a super-sized thunderstorm, with lightning flashing in the pre-dawn darkness, was not an experience Pete necessarily wanted to repeat. He was certain he would have lost his lunch if he'd had any... or breakfast.

Jerry kept up a constant patter—clearly he wasn't experiencing any discomfort—but Pete found himself wishing for an airsickness bag for the first time in his life. He blinked and called up a self-check menu on the EMT's ocular. The suit recommended a peristalsis inhibitor and mild muscle relaxant. He'd have to increase his vegetable and grain intake later or pay the consequences with gas and cramps, but it certainly made the ride less nauseating.

After they cleared the storm, Jinx poured on yet more speed, and it only took another thirty minutes until they were taxiing up to a hanger half a continent's width away from where they started. Base White was located in a rural region on the northeast coast of the principal continent on Akea, but Base Green was located on the edge of an urban center on the southwestern shore of that continent. The city itself had been hit by several cometary fragments more than a month ago, and the craters still glowed a dull orange as they continued to dissipate the massive heat of impact. A badly damaged and nearly abandoned metropolitan hospital had been located at this site. Repaired and expanded with multi-species medical teams, it now served to supplement the native Carico doctors and care staff.

After reporting to the chief of staff, Pete was ordered to assist in the overtaxed Emergency Department. It was hoped that the wide variety of injuries and ailments might trigger the ancient database built into his original EMT. The Carico were a "new" race in the experience of the Coalition, and neither the standard medical databases, nor the various EMTs in service, had been able to reveal specific medical information. The docs were falling back on standard practices and universal precautions in handing the Akeans.

The sun was just coming up as Pete reported to the Intake and Triage area. He scanned his first patient and waited for an identification by his EMT database. He was wearing the full suit, and the ocular displayed all of the information it had:

Species... unknown, humanoid, probable subtype 42xx

Height—one point three four meters,

Weight—62 kilograms

Sex—male (85% probability)

Compound fracture, left forearm (92% probability)—possible identity: left radius

Subcutaneous hematoma (35% probability). Internal bleeding - unknown

Internal injuries and/or organ damage—unknown

Hematology—unknown

Immunology—unknown

Unconscious (98% probability), Mental status—unknown

Dehydration and exposure (67% probability)

Shock (55% probability)

Volume expander—unknown risk, recommend Fluorodec minimal dosage

Rehydrate with local fluid sources

Nanites—contraindicated.

Pete had never seen the EMT respond with probabilities, instead of definite diagnosis and treatment orders; it was somewhat unsettling. He marked the chart for secondary priority—urgent but non-life-threatening injuries—and moved on to the next patient. He worked triage for the next four hours. After a brief meal break, he was sent to the emergency surgical bay—minus his full suit. We kept his gloves, and the nanite ocular interface. Again, it was hoped that exposure to the alien's internal organs (again, roughly human standard, but with at least three additional presumably endocrine organs, and no pancreas) would trigger recognition in the EMTs artificial intelligence.

Throughout all of this, Serena stood guard, either at the corner of the triage tent, or just outside the door to the surgical suite. She joined him at meal breaks, and while she didn't say much, Pete welcomed her company. The other doctors and medical staff were just too busy to do much more than acknowledge his presence.

"I don't understand it, Serena, how can the Carico not be in the EMT database?"

"Maybe they were completely unknown to the inventors?"

"Possibly. The colonel said that the Coalition didn't know of the Carico before they contacted Tomeral and Associates for assistance. Still, they have a stargate, so the Bith knew of them. The tech level of this world suggests they had communication with the rest of the galaxy."

"Maybe they invented the suits and hid their own data?"

"No, I don't think so. We're pretty sure humans invented the first EMT. The Mark XI's database lists Human as Species #1."

Serena grunted and went back to her salad of hydroponic greens and vat protein. Pete just nibbled on a protein bar. Back on Joth or Tretra, those were pretty tasteless, but these tasted like real food. It had been ten hours since Pete had reported for duty, and he had yet another four-hour shift to complete before finding his temporary quarters. He went to the dispenser and ordered coffee—triple strength—and sat back down to drink it in silence as he cross-referenced his EMT database with a network information search for more data on races similar to the Carico. He found a link that referenced some very old Earth idents that were labeled as "probably mythological." Called "large greys" and "small greys," they were similar, but didn't really fit the natives of Akea. The Carico had the same gray skin, large wide-set eyes and elongated heads, but also a pronounced midline ridge extending from the back of the head to the face, ending in a prominent nasal flare. Their mouths were slightly protuberant—not quite a muzzle, but not flat-faced like the "greys." The Carico were also covered in a fine fur that was gray with hints of iridescent blue and green. It was frustrating to be seemingly so close to a described species, and yet have no exact reference to the people he was trying to help.

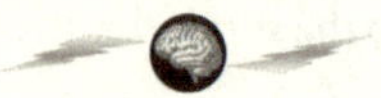

After a week of fourteen-to-eighteen-hour days providing triage, surgery and emergency care, Pete was called to report to the hospital chief of staff. Admiral Lurvel and Colonel Suminto were on video link and took turns quizzing Pete about the information obtained from his EMT that week.

After hearing Pete's report, the chief of staff addressed the others. "Gentle-beings, that's pretty much the same as what we got. There's no sense in keeping Doctor Emil here. We're well staffed and have people experienced with treating Carico now. I say we send him back to Base White to see what he can do with those research facilities."

Research facilities? Pete thought to himself. *There are research facilities? Are they medical? Perhaps I can find a clue there!*

As if reading his thoughts, Colonel Suminto nodded and answered Pete's unspoken question. "Indeed, we're sited near the Akean government's major scientific research institutions. There is a medical research facility about thirteen klicks from base. We've been excavating with some local help. Major Niveen is the lead on that project. I'll assign Pete to work with Eddie. How soon can you send him back?"

"Well, there's no urgency, so we won't subject him to the fighters, besides, that squadron is being reassigned to comet-chasing duty. You're too close for a ballistic hop, so we'll put him on the shuttle that's headed up to Mayaguez tonight and then back down to White in the morning. He can have a berth and get some sleep on the way."

Sleep. That would be nice!

The shuttle to Mayaguez left base Green at local midnight, but Pete was allowed to crawl into one of the bunk-like crew berths about an hour before departure. He slept through liftoff, rendezvous with the flagship, and through most of the unloading and reloading. Just before re-entry, he emerged from the tunnel-like sleeping space and took a seat in the passenger compartment next to Serena. She'd been sitting in that exact seat since he had gone to sleep—did she stay wake all night? She looked... pretty much the way she always did: Competent, alert, on guard. He looked at his own reflection on a seat-back screen. Nanites were crawling at the corners of his three eyes cleaning away dirt and dried mucus. He looked terrible—he'd need a 'fresher visit before he dared go back to the HQ.

It was noon before he reported back to the colonel. The entire operation was running short of time, but orders to get fed and cleaned up had come over his comm before they landed back at White. He entered the HQ facility to find only Eddie and the clerks. The colonel, Wally and Ralph were working a salvage and rescue site nearby.

"Good to see you, Rock Star! Did you have a nice beauty rest?" Eddie laughed and winked as he delivered the mild insult, so Pete didn't take it *too* seriously.

Pete yawned and stretched theatrically. "I don't know, Eddie, you ever sleep in one of those crew bunks? ... Oh, wait. You wouldn't fit, would you?"

"I can fit a Yalteen bunk just fine, but I know what you mean. Those things aren't much more than a shoulder-width tube." Eddie shuddered. "I'm not claustrophobic—can't be in this outfit—but I don't like them."

"Yeah. Same here. Okay, let me get some coffee and then you can point me to my next assignment."

"Here, I've got a cup for you already. Drink up and read this." Eddie handed over a slate with a diagram of a building.

"What's this ... underground? This is what, a bunker?"

"Nope, a lab. The Carico we talked to didn't know of it. It's old and buried underneath a farm about fifty klicks away. We've been doing ground-penetrating imaging to make sure we don't miss people in caves or bunkers. Colonel asked the folks at the main research complex, and they said there was a rumor of an old lab somewhere, but no-one knew the details."

"...and they found it?"

"Yes, they did, or rather, a team of mecha-suited marines found it while trying to evacuate some folks from a collapsed farm building. A Prithmar ended up falling down a hole and reported an underground structure. I think you might know him—a kid from Joth named Orlin."

Pete laughed. "Yes, that sounds like Orlin, always falling into trouble, but coming out the better for it."

"Indeed, the Admiral recommended a commendation, because he was in the process of rescuing one of the locals, who fell in first. He did rescue her, and had already gotten the family out. Once everyone was safe, he volunteered to explore, but the Colonel wanted Rescue Ops in there first, and then to get you down there." Eddie gave Pete a wry smile. "I hope you're rested; we're headed out in ten minutes."

"My EMT is right here..." Pete patted the wheeled case at his side. "... and I'm wearing everything else. Let's go!"

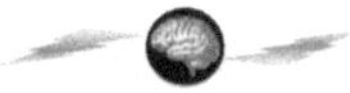

Although only fifty klicks away, it still took nearly an hour to reach the site via aircar. It was well away from the small urban concentration adjacent to base White, and up a box canyon filled with ranches and farms. "We think the lab is built under the mountain range. This access appears to be an emergency exit or air shaft," Colonel Suminto told Pete once they'd reached the site. "That makes this pretty tricky. There have been lots of ground movement and shocks. Ralph and Wally are currently in there mapping places where it's safe for us to access."

Pete and Eddie were taken over to view a couple of screens displaying scenes of the underground lab. One screen was fed by a camera attached to Wally's protective armor, while another showed the feed from Ralph's harness. There was a lot of debris on the floor, and a few places with cracked walls or ceiling, but for the most part, the facility seemed to be accessible.

Two other screens were clearly from larger sophonts, approximately Caldivar size, although bulked out much more in mechanical suits of armor. "One of those is Serena, the other's your friend, Orlin," Suminto said. "He asked for permission to remain with the survey once we gave approval. I'm having them scout out access to what we think are the main labs before I send you and Eddie in."

He was interrupted by a shout of surprise from the comm. Orlin's screen showed a new room, filled with unusual equipment, odd chairs... and a skeleton.

"That's—" Pete began.

"—Not a Carico," Eddie finished.

"Suit up, you two. Time to go in"

Pete and Eddie, in their respective EMTs with full armor supplement to protect their limbs and joints, were met by Ralph, who led them to where Orlin and Serena guarded the entrance to the lab.

"The ceiling's not particularly stable, so the two heavies are going to play 'Atlas' and make sure the sky doesn't fall on you." Ralph yipped a bit in laughter, then continued. "Seriously, they are your rescue. Try not to move anything that is next to a supporting wall or touching the ceiling. I know we can't convince you not to touch anything, but just use some common sense. If the wall or ceiling collapses, Wally and I are going to have to dig you out, and it takes *ages* to get the dust out of my fur!" Pete laughed, but assured Ralph that he would be careful.

The room was indeed a lab, and there were not one, but two skeletons in the room. The first was seated in a chair, the other laid out on a medical or surgical platform. The one on the table was—mostly—Carico, but with a more of a snout shape to the skull, and a vestigial tail extending from the bottom of the vertebral column.

The other skeleton, though, was amazing! If standing, it would be as tall as Eddie—over two meters in height. It was bipedal with very long limbs and short torso. The hips were positioned such that the legs would contribute more than half the total height of the creature, while the long arms extended almost to the knees. Most amazing was a humanoid skull with a flat face and very long cranium that extended back much further than a human.

Pete had seen this creature lately. The EMT reported:

Species... 5. "Large Grey"
Deceased.
Height—two point three meters,
Weight (estimated)—80 kilograms
Sex—female (62% probability)

"Not so mythological after all." Pete muttered to himself.

"What was that, Captain Emil? You have an identification?" Suminto asked over the comm.

"Yes, sir. The EMT database identifies the seated skeleton as a 'Large Grey,' Species number 5 in the database. I read that they are considered to be a myth."

"Interesting. Number five, eh? This is a very ancient species."

"Yes, sir." Pete paused a moment. "Sir, do we have any idea how old this installation is?"

"I think I can answer that," Eddie responded. He was in the next room over, and Pete could see him holding up a dust-encrusted instrument in his left hand, pointing sensors at it with his upper right hand, and tracing an engraving on the bottom surface with his lower right hand. "This is a pre-gate Earth language, and my instruments suggest it's about seven thousand years old."

"But this facility can't be that old... can it?"

"No, the construction reads out as about two-to-three-thousand years old."

"So, either someone was collecting old lab equipment, or ... *using* old equipment?"

The comm crackled. "Hey guys, we're starting to get some indications of movement. Just being in there seems to have caused something to shift." That was Orlin. Pete had spoken only very briefly with him when he entered the facility. He looked around and could see some streams of dust and dirt coming down from the ceiling.

"Confirmed, it's unstable. Finish taking pictures and get out of there," Suminto said.

"ALERT. ALERT. Meteor Swarm Alert."

A synthesized voice came over the comms and could be heard echoing from locations and outside.

"This is an Emergency Alert over Coalition and local channels. SKYWATCH has confirmed a meteor swarm impact zone extending fifty kilometers either side of a line extending from forty-two point six-seven north latitude, seventy-three point eight-eight west longitude, to forty-four point two-seven north latitude by seventy-two point six-zero west longitude. Expect impacts of molten debris ranging

from point one to two point zero meters in size. Seek immediate cover and avoid structures in danger of collapse. Ground all aircraft and take immediate cover."

The message repeated several times. Pete checked the compact slate attached to his left arm. The impact zone was approximately one-hundred by one-fifty kilometers, and almost exactly on their current location! Before he could move he felt the ground jolt. The comm emitted a sharp squeal, but cut off as Serena's agitated voice came over the local comm circuit. "Major, Captain, Sergeant Ralph, get out of there. We had an impact almost on top of the Command Center vehicle. It's been tossed and overturned. Wally and I are going over to check it out. Lieutenant Orlin will keep your route open. Get up and to the surface, that complex is ripe for cave-in."

There was another impact shock, and Pete lost his balance. He put out a hand to stop his fall and inadvertently touched the skeleton on what he'd come to think of as an examination table. Suddenly, the ocular display started to scroll text.

Species... 114. "Ocaricoso"

Deceased.

Height—one point one meters.

Weight (estimated)—36 kilograms

Sex—female (79% probability)

Age at death—thirteen years

Cause of death—agathic decay, accelerated aging

Probability of epigenetic modification—100%

The display paused for a moment, then the next row began to blink as additional text filled the display.

UPDATE PENDING.

Redesignating unknown species as 114 uplift variant

New Designation Species 114.1X—uplifted.

Emergency Medical Tool network update push pending connection.

Network connection... paused

Master server core detected,

Beginning download.

Download completed... resuming EMT network push.
External link authorized and activated.
CASE INDIGO – CASE INDIGO – CASE INDIGO. EMT override
Five-Alpha, priority one. DANGER! EXTREME DANGER! Facility Collapse
Imminent!
Emergency core dump in process.

Ralph yipped in surprise. "Uh, Pete, what did you do? These machines are all starting to light up!" There was a thud, and Eddie could be heard cursing in Eitom in the background.

"Captain! What the *hell* did you do? This damned machine turned on and shocked me, causing me to drop it on my foot!"

Pete was completely unable to respond, because his EMT display stopped scrolling text, everything went blank, and the suit became rigid. Pete was unable to move, unable to see through his nanite ocular (or at all, since his helmet-mounted lights turned off) and the leg and arm sleeves puffed up to immobilize him. He tried to waddle, but the overlapping armor at shoulders and hips seemed to have locked in place.

All he could do was shout. "My EMT has shut down and locked me in place. Leave me and get out of here. I'll try to take it off and join you."

"Not without help, you're not." Eddie came in to the room. Clearly his EMT was still functional. "Ralph, head to the entrance and tell the marine we'll be late."

Ralph yipped in acknowledgement and took off on all fours.

"*Dammit*, Pete, what did you do?" Eddie started pulling at the sleeves, but Pete's suit seemed to be locked together at the now-inflexible joints.

After several minutes of trying in vain to remove the suit, Eddie was ready to pick Pete up and carry him to the exit. They could here yipping as Ralph returned.

"Sergeant, you were supposed to get out of here." A vibration in the floor indicated the approach of one of the marine mecha.

"You can't carry him, but I can, Major." Orlin had come into the complex to retrieve his friend. "No man—or Caldivar—left behind, sir!"

"I'm not going to argue, Lieutenant. Pick him up and let's go."

"No!" Pete protested. "My suit was communicating with these machines! I can't leave!" There was another distant impact, and a portion of the ceiling fell on the examining table, shattering the skeleton that his suit had briefly identified as *Ocaricoso*. "There's a server here somewhere and we need to find it."

"No, Captain, we're going. Pick him up, marine, we're going now."

Pete felt tethers being attached to his limbs, and then he was picked up and slung across Orlin's back. Ralph led the way as the four of them moved as quickly as they could through the collapsing underground facility. He would have yelled and protested, but in his heart, he knew his Eddie was right.

At the entrance, Orlin attached everyone to a thick cable running down the center, touched a control on his wrist, and they were all yanked from their feet and hauled to the surface. A couple of technicians tending the equipment at the wellhead helped them off to the side and disconnected the lift cable. The narrow walls at the head of the canyon would be less prone to collapse, so the entire team headed for shelter. Pete was still slung across the back of Orlin's mecha, and he saw a large cloud of dust and dirt rising from the wellhead.

They made a shelter at the narrowest part of the canyon—the ceiling was basically Orlin's mecha, supplemented by an emergency survival tent found in one of the technician's packs. There were still minor rock falls with each impact, but they were not in immediate danger of being buried or hit. They stayed sheltered in place for over an hour, until the emergency comm announced that the meteor shower was over.

A few minutes later, they saw Serena coming their way, helping a limping Colonel Suminto and carrying Wally under one arm. They were greeted with relief and a bit of nervous laughter, but Pete just sat silently. His EMT was dead, and he had no idea what caused it, other than the fact that it had identified a new species right before everything went wrong.

He'd finally managed to get his helmet off with Eddie and Serena's help, and went to wipe the dead nanites off of his face when he noticed that the ocular was not completely black. There was a single red dot, and as he watched, it gradually faded to orange, then yellow, then green.

A second green dot appeared next to the first, then a third, then a fourth.

"Hey, uh, guys? Colonel? I think my EMT is booting back up."

Eddie came over to look and said, "Yes, I can see a line of dots on your chest display. Huh, now there's words, but it's that weird old-earth script."

Pete's ocular showed the same script. Fortunately, he'd learned to read it many years ago courtesy of a translation overlay used to view the original displays. "It says 'Memory usage 99.9% - add external storage.'"

"Hey, tech, you got a memory cube in that backpack of yours?" Eddie asked the technician who'd had the survival tent.

The answer was no, but Serena offered to go back the command vehicle and retrieve supplies. With Orlin's help, she got it right-side up and running, and a few minutes later they heard the hum and crunch of the command vehicle approaching on ground wheels as Serena brought it back to their temporary camp.

Pete's EMT did not continue its boot-up process not until a technician came back with a storage cube and plugged it into a receptacle on Pete's clamshell. The memory usage message went away, and the green dots continued to fill the display. After another twenty minutes, the suit asked for another storage unit. In all, they filled five storage cubes before the display was filled with green dots, then cleared.

The familiar start-up symbols filled his ocular, quickly replaced by a message Pete had never seen before.

> *Founder diagnostic interrupt encountered.*
> *Offline storage complete.*
> *Heuristic content rebuild pending transfer to master server.*
> *System broadcast awaiting superuser credentials.*
> *Local broadcast pending playback.*
> *Initiate playback? (Y/N)*

"Colonel? My suit seems to want to play a message. It says it encountered a 'Founder diagnostic' and has stored 'heuristic content' on those offline storage cubes."

"Heuristic? Oh, we're going to need to buck that all the way to President Tomeral. His AI, Jayneen, probably needs to analyze those before we dare plug them into anything. Go ahead and play the message, though. See if you can broadcast it."

Pete queried his EMT, and it confirmed that it could broadcast using nanites to form Tri-Vee pixels. Once he acknowledged playback, an image started to form in the middle of their group. The figure was nearly identical to the 'mythological Large Grey' he'd seen in his searches.

Much to their surprise, when it spoke, each of them heard it in their species' native language. Pete heard in in Caldi-high, the technical language, which surprised him, since Caldi-low was used as the universal communications medium.

"Sophonts. If you are viewing this, you have found my laboratory. Hopefully I have finished my work.

"Call me Ozmin. It is not my name, but one you can all understand and pronounce. I have been working on the Ocaricoso—number one-hundred fourteen in my catalog. A natural disaster changed their genetic structure, causing them to age very fast, and they are in danger of extinction. They have such beautiful artworks, poetry, and music, but all will be lost if I cannot restore their lifespan and reproductive ability.

"I fear that I may have to introduce so many changes that they will be unrecognizable. I only hope that in so doing, I do not affect their art.

"I offer to you a gift. The servers in this laboratory are filled with all of my data, but also all of the art I have been able to collect. Look upon my works and rejoice, for I dare not allow such as these to be lost for all eternity!"

"So, he succeeded," Harmon Tomeral said.

Pete was a bit nervous being in the compartment with President Tomeral and his top assistants. The AI Jayneen had just finished presenting her analysis of the memory cubes—they were exactly what the recording said. The Salvage System President and Coalition Commander had invited Admiral Lurvel, Colonel Suminto and his team to the briefing and was now open to comments.

"As far as we can tell," the admiral replied. "We have managed to shelter most of the population of Akea, and swept the system of the worst of the cometary fragments. The EMTs all updated even before Colonel Suminto's team got back in contact with us. With the updated EMT database, we can see that the Carico are indeed genetically derived from the Ocaricoso, only with a one-hundred-year lifespan and an effective thirty-year reproductive range. The data from the laboratory suggests that this was all Ozmin's work, since the Ocaricoso only lived twenty years and didn't become fertile until a year before they died of old age."

Eddie and Pete had been busy examining as much of the data as possible once it had been certified not to pose a cyber-security risk.

The Admiral turned to Pete. He knew what was coming, because they had been over it so many times, but he knew they needed to repeat it for the coalition leader. "And it was specifically your suit that triggered the data."

"Yes, sir. Eddie—um, I mean Major Niveen, sir—was in the lab before I was, and he was within visual range when my EMT received the download." Pete responded, then took a sip of water to soothe his very dry throat. It wasn't his first time coming under the scrutiny of President Tomeral, but he had hoped not to have it happen again.

"You do seem to make interesting finds, Doctor Emil. First the EMT, then a kidnapped heiress, now the laboratory of one of the individuals who likely invented that suit."

"Yes sir." It was all Pete could get out without risking a coughing fit. It had been two months, but he still felt as if he was breathing the dusty air of the laboratory.

Harmon smiled. "Be at ease, son. That's a compliment. I understand you have to finish your residency, but I think we'll be talking again."

The President invited them all to remain and enjoy a good meal and hospitality, but all Pete could think of was that he was overdue writing to his mom and Susa. He'd have to break it to her gently that he'd be on Salvage for quite a few more years. It would be all he could do to keep her from insisting on joining him while he was still going to be too busy to spend any time with her.

He was so preoccupied with his thoughts that he didn't even realize Colonel Suminto was standing next to him until his commanding officer leaned over to whisper in his ear. "Tell the young lady to come to Salvage, Major Emil. Majors can marry, after all!"

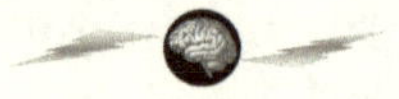

Acknowledgements

I'd like to thank Kevin Steverson for the opportunity to play in his Salvage Title universe. When I first read the titular book, and it's first two sequels, I was struck by how similar it felt to some of the classic Boy Scout stories I'd read when I was younger. I always wanted to play in that sandbox, so when offered the chance to contribute to Salvage Conquest, I jumped at the chance and created Pete, Orlin, Jerry, and Jinx as essentially young Scouts in a Sci-Fi setting. With the opportunity to write more stories, I stuck with the quartet, and concentrated on Pete Ekil and his dream of becoming a doctor.

So here, for the first time in one place, are the three Petekil Ekil stories I contributed to the Salvage Title Universe. I want to especially thank Sandra Medlock for editorial assistance, as well as William Alan Webb and Jamie Ibson for cover and formatting assistance and advice. To the entire Peacemaker Cantina—I can't think of a better, more supportive, and more educational group of writers. To Chris Kennedy, thanks for bringing us all together and giving me a chance at my first independent publications.

About the Author

Dr. Robert E. Hampson is a Neuroscientist and author. By day, he is a professor at Wake Forest School of Medicine, studying how our brains encode memory. By night, he writes military, adventure and hard-science Science Fiction as well as nonfiction articles explaining science to the general public.

Robert Hampson's SF writing career began with "They Also Serve," a short story in Riding the Red Horse, published in 2015. That story became the foundation of his first solo novel The Human Side, in 2020. He has three collaborative novels with Sandra Medlock, Chris Kennedy and Casey Moores in the "Wrogul's Oath" arc of the popular Four Horsemen Universe. A final book in this arc is expected in late 2023.

Rob's latest novel is *The Moon and the Desert,* an updated retelling of The Six Million Dollar Man. In addition to novels, he has co-edited two anthologies, and published more than 25 works of short fiction (some written as "Tedd Roberts"). He is also a regular contributor of nonfiction articles for science fiction readers, with more than 15 articles published. One of the articles, "Why Science is Never Settled," was nominated for the Hugo Award in 2015 as Best Related Work. Hampson has sequels in the works to both solo novels, the Wrogul's Oath, and The Founder Effect anthology.

Dr. Hampson's forty-year scientific career has ranged from studying the effects of commonly abused drugs on memory, to the effects of space radiation on the brain. His current work, as lead scientist for Braingrade, Inc., is developing a medical device to restore human memory function damaged by injury or disease. He is also a professor of physiology/pharmacology and neurology at

Wake Forest School of Medicine where he teaches regularly in the neuroscience and biomedical graduate curriculum. He also developed and teaches a course on Communicating Science, in which young scientists practice writing for—and speaking to—the general public. He is a scientific journal editor; a reviewer for dozens of journals and research agencies; has been interviewed on his research by newspapers, radio and TV; a consultant to TV and game producers, defense contractors, and authors. He has published more than 175 peer-reviewed scientific articles.

Hampson graduated in 1988 with a PhD from the Bowman Gray School of Medicine of Wake Forest University in Winston-Salem, NC. He has worked as a newspaper carrier, greeting card merchandizer, computer data entry operator and programmer, and laboratory technician, and lived in Pennsylvania, Texas, and North Carolina. He now lives in the Piedmont of North Carolina with his wife, Ruann.

Robert E. Hampson is available as a consultant through SIGMA — the Science Fiction Think Tank and the Science and Entertainment Exchange (a service of the National Academy of Sciences). His website is .

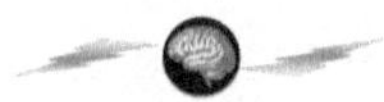

Books by Robert E. Hampson

The Moon and the Desert - Baen Books

ISBN 978-1-982192-49-5

What would it really take to make the Six Million Dollar Man? a medical thriller on earth and in space!

Glenn Armstrong Shepard had his sights set on going to Mars as a flight surgeon, but a training accident on the Moon left him crippled. Now he has a new plan: to be fitted with bionic prosthetics and come back even stronger.

Fate and the Space Force have other plans, and Glenn is grounded. Another doctor—his ex-fiancée—takes his place, and Glenn will have to fight to prove he can be an astronaut once more. . . .

The Human Side - Theogony Books

ISBN 978-1-648550-70-6

Is it an asteroid...or a weapon?

An asteroid headed toward Earth was not unexpected; multiple asteroids were a different story. And, when the "rock-throwing aliens" finally appeared, the people of Earth had to deal with a new type of war, where an enemy with powerful weapons held the high ground of space.

Dr. Tobias Greene felt guilty over patching up soldiers only to have them return to battle—until learning that his work was essential to the survival of the human race.

Master Sergeant Martin was a combat medic, trying to do his job and save as many as he could.

Lab Technician Kat Smith was forced out of her home and away from friends and family by the alien attacks. Her work was important, but would it be enough?

Jan and Li Janacek were trapped in New Mexico with their son, daughter, and eight other teens. They needed to get home...but home was no longer there.

For Arielle French, the aliens' arrival was everything she had predicted, until they attacked. Had she misunderstood their motives, or was it all the fault of the humans who failed to behave the way the aliens expected?

Technical breakthroughs might allow humans to resist the worst the "Rockers" could throw at them. But even if they could level the battlefield, though, would there be enough time left for Earth to show the Rockers what was really on the Human Side?

The Founder Effect - Anthology (edited with Sandra L. Medlock) - Baen Books

ISBN 978-1-982125-09-7

AWARD-WINNING AND BEST-SELLING AUTHORS CON-TRIBUTE NEW STORIES: All-new fiction from Dragon Award winner and

New York Times best-selling author David Weber, Dragon Award nominee D
.J. Butler, best seller Jody Lynn Nye, indie best sellers Chris Kennedy and Mark
Wandrey, and more. Also featuring an introduction by multi-award-winning
and New York Times best-selling author Larry Correia.

It is 2185 CE. Humans now live throughout the Solar System, but their most
ambitious adventure is about to begin. The starship Victoria will carry over
10,000 colonists to a new world outside the Solar System. The larger-than-life
exploits of those colonists will become legendary. The colonists will build a
new civilization, and the actions of a few individuals will become famous—and
infamous—forever marking their new colony with the Founder Effect.

Contributors: Larry Correia, Mark H. Wandrey, Les Johnson, Christopher
L. Smith, David Weber, Daniel M. Hoyt, Brad R. Torgersen, Monalisa Foster,
Sarah A. Hoyt, Chris Kennedy, Vivienne Raper, Jody Lynn Nye, Brent M.
Roeder, Catherine L. Smith, Philip Wohlrab, D.J. Butler

Stellaris: People of the Stars - Anthology (edited with Les Johnson) - Baen Books

ISBN 978-1-481484-25-1

NEW STORIES AND ESSAYS FROM TOP AUTHORS AND EXPERT
SCIENTISTS. Explorations of how interstellar travel may affect humanity by
best-selling authors and scientists.

The stars will change us.

STELLARIS: PEOPLE OF THE STARS is a collection of original science
fiction stories and nonfiction essays speculating about humanity's far-term ex-
pansion into the universe beyond the limits of our solar system—with an em-
phasis on the changes humans will undergo as a species as we make this happen.
Is interstellar travel so far beyond our current imaginings that it will take a

fundamental transformation of humanity in order to make it possible? And, if so, will we remain Homo sapiens or become a new and unique species—Homo stellaris (the People of the Stars)?

Herein are original science fiction stories by award-winning authors such as Kevin J. Anderson, William Ledbetter, Todd McCaffrey and Sarah A. Hoyt, supplemented by accessible nonfiction essays describing the science behind the fiction from people who should know—Sir Martin Rees (Astronomer Royal of the United Kingdom), Mark Shelhamer (Chief Scientist for the NASA's Human Research Program), and more.

This collection of original stories and essays was inspired by a gathering of scientists, science fiction authors, and futurists at a series of annual meetings held by the Tennessee Valley Interstellar Workshop. Let their speculations, imaginations and boundless sense of what's possible take your own journey beyond the edge of the solar system in STELLARIS: PEOPLE OF THE STARS!

Stories and Provocative Speculation from:

Sir Martin Rees, Kevin J. Anderson, Sarah A. Hoyt, Mike Massa, William Ledbetter, Todd McCaffrey, Kacey Ezell and Philip Wohlrab, Dan Hoyt, Les Johnson, Robert E. Hampson, Mark Shelhamer, Brent Roeder, Jim Beall, Cathe Smith

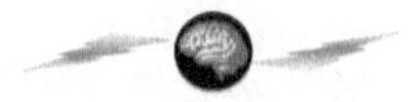

The Wrogul's Oath

Four Horsemen Universe

Books by Robert E. Hampson and Sandra L. Medlock

Do No Harm (Robert E. Hampson and Chris Kennedy with Sandra L. Medlock)

ISBN 978-1-950420-11-7

When Todd's critically damaged ship dropped out of hyperspace near the Human colony world of Azure, he had no memory of his past. He didn't know who he was, or even what he was, and the Humans didn't either. That didn't stop the colonists of Azure—they took him in, anyway...even though they didn't understand how he could do some of the things he could do.

Todd and his descendants consider themselves Human—eight armed and water-breathing—but Human, nonetheless. After seventy years living among Humans, Todd's descendants are going back out into the Union to make their mark—from fifteen-year-old Verne, who's a little short to be a mercenary, to Harryhausen, who wants to be the most famous PI in the galaxy. Eventually they learn that the rest of the Galactic Union knows them as Wrogul, intelligent octopus-like beings known for science and the ability to perform surgery like no other race can.

These Wrogul do more than just practice medicine, but they still intend to do no harm. Unfortunately, the Humans, whether they have two arms or eight, have powerful enemies... and the Wrogul may have no choice.

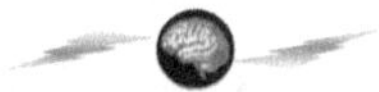

And Break It Not (Robert E. Hampson and Sandra L. Medlock)

ISBN 978-1-648551-92-5

The planet of Azure is nearly idyllic—there is a high standard of living, industry is booming, and the two races—Human and Wrogul—get along well with each other most days.

But underneath it all, there is tension between the races. Despite having no reason for it, the Humans don't always trust the Wrogul, and there is a faction within the Wrogul community that doesn't want its young growing up "Human."

When a large group of Wrogul move into the ocean and strange things begin happening—weird lights seen in the depths and sabotage at the mariculture stations—the Human's distrust becomes outright suspicion of treachery.

As things spiral out of control, another force enters the system—a group ostensibly sent by the UN on Earth to inspect the crops being grown on Azure—which threatens to destroy everything the Humans and Wrogul have worked for.

While the Wrogul still intend to do no harm, the Humans have powerful enemies in the galaxy, and, this time, the Wrogul may have no choice about whether to join the front lines with their Human friends. Will the threat of a common enemy break the relationship between the Humans and Wrogul...or break it not?

As My Witnesses (Sandra L. Medlock and Casey Moores with Robert E. Hampson)

ISBN 978-1-648554-17-9

Azure Colony avoided the larger conflicts of the Omega War and Guild Wars, only to fall prey to rogue mercenaries. Now they're rebuilding, but strange forces are at work. New friends on the ground and mysterious lights in the sky promise "interesting times" for the Humans and hyper-intelligent Wrogul of Azure.

Meanwhile, mercenary leader Verne and Peacemaker Harryhausen resume their search for the ancestral home of Azure's Wrogul. They encounter distrust, deceit, and misdirection from the all-powerful guilds, but they manage to learn of sightings of Wrogul-like aliens. Their strongest lead takes them to a forgotten system where a lost Human colony coexists with a strange alien race with remarkable similarities to the Wrogul.

But when they find the colony is in the middle of a civil war, they're forced to make a choice—do they choose sides or stand by while the colonists slaughter each other?

This I Swear (Sandra L. Medlock with Casey Moores and Robert E. Hampson)

Forthcoming in 2023 - the surprising conclusion to Todd's search for his ancestors.

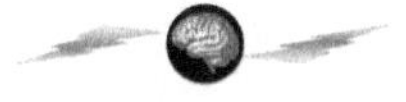

9 781961 172098